MONARCH
of
DEADMAN BAY

OTHER TITLES BY ROGER A. CARAS
AVAILABLE IN BISON BOOK EDITIONS

The Custer Wolf:
Biography of an American Renegade

Panther!

MONARCH
of
DEADMAN BAY

*The Life and Death
of a Kodiak Bear*

by ROGER A. CARAS

Illustrations by Charles Fracé

University of Nebraska Press
Lincoln

First Bison Book printing: 1990
Most recent printing indicated by the last digit below:
10   9   8   7   6   5   4   3   2   1

Library of Congress Cataloging-in-Publication Data
Caras, Roger A.
Monarch of Deadman Bay: the life and death of a Kodiak bear /
by Roger A. Caras; [illustrations by Charles Fracé].
p.   cm.
Reprint. Originally published: 1st ed. Boston: Little, Brown,
c1969.
ISBN 0-8032-6337-6
1. Kodiak bear.   2. Natural history—Alaska—Kodiak Island.
I. Title.
QL795.B4C28   1990
599.74'446—dc20
90-12312   CIP

Reprinted by arrangement with Roger A. Caras

∞

For Pamela and Clay . . .
who understand so much

MONARCH
of
DEADMAN BAY

 I.

KODIAK ISLAND, ALL 3,465 SQUARE MILES OF IT, HUDDLES
in the northern sector of the great Alaskan Bay like an
enormous amoeba waiting to envelop the smaller islands
of the archipelago that bears this island's name. Cut off
from the Arctic Ocean by the Alaskan Peninsula, Kodiak
Island is under the comparatively mild spell of temperate
southeastern Alaska rather than in the harsher grasp of
the land of Eskimos and polar bears.

One hundred and three miles long, fifty-seven miles
wide, rain-drenched for much of the year, the Island is

situated between 56° 40′ and 58° north latitude, 152° and 155° west longitude. High in the east and covered with conifer and hardwood forests of Sitka spruce and cotton-woods, the Island descends over four thousand feet toward the tundrous west with its uniform cover of muskeg grass. Here only scattered clumps of alders break the monotony.

It is a wild land. Although long settled it has never been tamed. The city of Kodiak, huddling in the north-eastern part of the Island, is the sixth largest settlement in Alaska and dates from 1794, when it was the capital of Russian America. Yet only a few miles away it is possible for even an experienced woodsman to get hopelessly lost in a tangle of land that rises and falls like a stormy sea.

This blue-gray land, serenaded by a chorus of gulls a million strong, has over a thousand miles of coastline that resembles, often enough, Norway's fjord-indented shores. The treacherous Shelikof Strait to the north separates the Island from the great land mass of the Alaskan Peninsula by thirty miles. A graveyard for un-wary sailors, these waters and those along the Island's other shores roll inward in high, fast tides that swallow the rocky beaches and seaweed flats in greedy gulps. Kodiak Island's granite, slate and even sandstone have so far withstood the sea's intrusion. It owes its shape and the long shadows of its ragged hills to the carving power of prehistoric sheets of glacial ice.

A history measured in millions of years, with the intermingling influences of sea and quake, glacier and wind, makes it hard to tell how a given feature of the land was formed. It may have once been two islands, for the largest fjord to slash her coast, Uyak or Windy Bay, west of the Island's middle in the north, cuts forty miles inland and all but meets Deadman Bay in the south.

Kodiak Island shows many scars, only the least of which were made by man. The quarries that have been cut into her hills, the roads on their sides and the light cosmetic touches to her natural bays are of little account. More momentous things have shaped this land. From June 6 to June 8 in 1912, Mount Novarupta on the Alaskan Peninsula to the north showered millions of tons of raw volcanic ash on Kodiak Island, in many places to a depth of twelve or more inches. All the changes wrought by all the men who have ever stepped ashore on this island are as nothing compared with the force let loose upon it in those few hours.

When the winds are high, and they often are, and when the sea is angry with the land, rain does not simply fall on Kodiak Island; it is hurled against this intruder in the sea like shrapnel. Fog banks engulf her like living things. This island is like a ship at sea, and often she sails uneasily through unaccountable weather fronts. There are days, though, when the land sails out of the mists and drifts on calm and sunlit waters. On such days men know why they have come to this place.

Such a land as this, raw one moment and steaming the next, provides a garden in which giants can grow.

The female bear eased slowly into the clearing on the south side of the hill. She was seven years old and had attained her maximum growth. Her head and body together were over seven feet long and when she stood square on her pillar-thick legs she was over four feet at the shoulders. She weighed about seven hundred pounds. Since it was still mid-May her lustrous golden bronze coat was prime. Only a few — perhaps five or six percent — of the bears on the Island had coats of this color. In another six weeks she would be ragged from the shedding and rubbing that would continue through August. Still fresh from her winter's rest, however, her fur was thick and lush.

Her humped shoulders distinctive as she stood, she rotated her head on her short, muscular neck, her nose pointing straight up. Her small, close-set eyes could tell her little, but her keen ears and sensitive nose would report most of what she had to know. The unrelenting demands of survival had sorted these things out over thousands of centuries of evolution.

Her ears, small, round and erect, set far apart on her broad skull, twitched as a downy woodpecker chinked metallically in a tree nearby. Her lips rolled back and she woofed hoarsely. Her somewhat pointed jaws, loosely articulated for grinding vegetation, moved easily and she stooped to graze on some meadow barley, then shuffled forward to where the favored bluejoint grew. These preferred grazing plants and others as well, beach rye, the sedges, nettle and seacoast angelica, had brought the sow down from the mountains for the first phase of her spring feast.

She stopped often to listen, for she was seeking more

than food. The preceding summer she had had cubs of a previous mating still with her and their sucking stimulus had inhibited ovulation. Free now, and alone once again, her seasonal estrus had begun. Descending ova were ready for fertilization and the sow's behavior would be dictated by the compelling instinct to mate again. Nature, intent on the propagation of her wonders, arranged such matters carefully.

Abruptly the sow stopped grazing, raised her head, sniffed, woofed softly, then bawled. Her call ended in a whine that mixed intricately with a loud chopping of her jaws. Although she could not pick out his shape she knew a boar stood back among the trees examining those of her secrets that could be wind-borne. The mating play had begun and would not be concluded until nature had assured herself of another generation of brown bear cubs. These two giants had survived many dangers and difficulties; the price of their survival was more of their kind.

The female stood in the middle of the clearing, woofing hoarsely and occasionally whining. The male moved toward her cautiously. He had been following her for hours. His nose told him she was in heat and ready to break her solitude. Still, instinctively, he knew that if he was wrong and if this was a sow with cubs, he could expect an explosive reaction to his approach. Males are often cannibalistic toward cubs, their own as well as those of other boars, and females can be quick and savage in defense of their offspring.

The big chocolate boar, more typical of brown bear

color than the bronze sow, tested the wind continuously as he shuffled toward his prospective mate. If she was the sow who had laid down the tantalizing trail, her standing fast in the clearing was a good sign. If she was a different animal, it was a dangerous situation, because it meant she had decided to fight. Few females will stand up to a boar, but those that do have the advantage of a determination more fierce than a male's hunger for cub flesh.

Satisfied at last that this was the sow he had been following, having sorted her out from the scents of other bears that had passed through the clearing earlier in the day, he quickened his gait.

As they came together they woofed and rubbed noses in a gesture surprisingly gentle for such formidable animals. In a few minutes they were feeding side by side in a most sociable manner. In fact, only on this occasion would either of them seek out or even tolerate the company of another mature bear. Between matings they lived solitary and short-tempered existences.

There was no breeding that day or the next, the time being spent in companionable foraging. Late the following afternoon, however, the male began to exhibit more precise interest in the sow and she was obliged on several occasions to plunk her ample bottom down hard to stop the rude intrusions of his nose. He was becoming more persistent. She was slow to respond but the critical business which they were about had softened their dispositions and there was no brawling. That would come later.

On their second night together the pair did not bed down apart as they had done the night before. There was a growing intimacy and as they lay close in the dark on the side of the hill they nibbled at each other's lips and occasionally slapped each other with ponderous paws. Their dark brown claws, recurved, strong and ever available, had grown long during the winter denning and were not yet worn down. They were not brought into play, though, and the slapping was good-natured with broad, plantigrade feet. Paws that could smash small trees with a single blow were used for caressing, and so the night passed.

There seemed to be an understanding reached during the playful hours of the second night. On the morning of their third day the sow submitted easily as the great boar covered her. The surrounding woods echoed with the wonderful range of their voices. They came apart after a few minutes and began to feed on tender spring plants almost immediately. Later that afternoon, when the boar covered her with his great bulk a second time, they remained locked together for nearly an hour. Erectile nodes blocked the vagina and kept the precious sperm from being lost.

During the days that followed they copulated several times more. When the sow showed signs of wanting to break loose, the male would plant his paws in front of her hips with his head lying along her neck. Her wriggling was to no avail and only when she began to whip her head back and forth and make violent chomping sounds with her jaws, only when he could sense her mounting anger, would he release her. By the end of the first week she was far less tolerant of the male's insistent appetite.

Early in the second week the female watched with

marked indifference as the boar, an experienced warrior of eleven breeding seasons, chased a smaller male away after giving him a vicious beating. The pair had been feeding apart for several hours each day since the end of the first week and the young male had approached the bronze sow as she grazed alone on an easy slope. The sudden appearance of the older boar on a ridge above startled the less experienced male, who was soon routed. The hunter who was to take the smaller boar's life the following year would wonder how he came to be missing an ear.

The big male returned to the female's side to find no recognition of his valiant deeds. Whether to reprimand her, or just because the fray had shortened his temper, the boar cuffed his mate rather too violently and she ran off and sat down among some nearby trees to sulk. It was two days before he saw her again. When they met she allowed him to mount her for the last time. During the ensuing ten days they met often, fed together for hours on end, and even bedded down close to each other on several occasions, but their sexual interest in each other had all but evaporated. At any time now their innate need for solitude would repossess them and they would drift apart permanently.

In the middle of the fourth week they met for a brief hour of feeding, but that part of them that demanded solitude had gained dominance over their sexual pattern, and they dissolved their union without ceremony.

The next morning found the sow moving in a westerly direction. Two fertilized eggs inside her uterus had already started to develop but would undergo a dormant stage before becoming implanted. Although the month was June it would not be until December that the embryos, potentially great beasts that could weigh almost three quarters of a ton, would be three quarters of an inch long. Since nature had ordained that all bear cubs around the world be born during the last week in January or the first week in February, the delay in development was essential to the schedule.

Alone, now, and hostile to all other bears, cubs and adults alike, the sow moved off and began feeding in earnest. The year was 1950 but it could have been any one of the four and a half million that have passed since the Pleistocene, when the species emerged. Its origin is traceable to a time twenty million years ago when *Hemicyon*, part dog, part bear, stalked lesser Miocene fauna. The more direct ancestor of the species was *Uasavus*, a wolf-sized bear of Europe as it was fifteen million years ago. A few million years later, in the Pliocene era, *Ursus arctos*, the European brown bear, was on the scene and from it descended all the brown bears and grizzlies whose ranges circle the globe in the Northern Hemisphere. When man was still only a vague potential in an ape's loins, the basis of the bears' mating ritual was already millions of years old. The precision of its formula stems from that antiquity. Although the bear is an intelligent and adaptable creature, in matters as critical as this neither of these two qualities is required. Nature does not trust such basics to choice. In mating the bear is guided by instinct; its behavior is rigidly controlled.

 2.

THERE WAS NO SPECIFIC PLAN TO THE SOW'S GENERAL movement toward the west and south. She had moved down into the valley from her winter denning site, mated, and was now continuing her wandering without conscious concern for her goal. She was biding her time before the start of the salmon run that would take her to certain streams in the area. Spring was passing into summer with its inevitable battle of white versus green and brown. White would lose and retreat to the highest hills in the east and north. The blue lupine, the white windflower, ragwort, four species of orchids, yellow violets, blue irises, flowers shaped like bells and others like stars, flowers sweet and some with poisonous roots, grew in wild profusion. Color was creeping back into the land and overhead the activities of the birds became frenetic.

Without regard for the havoc she created, the sow wandered from larder to larder. Birds challenged her whenever she passed a nest or brushed against a favored tree. Year-round residents, the magpie, black-capped chickadee, the varied thrush and the crossbill, cocked their heads and worried about her size. Summer visitors, violet-green swallows, the hermit thrush, pine grosbeaks, redpolls, and dozens more that had been goaded into their perilous journey to the Island by a fury and drive they could not understand, discussed her every move. As she moved by day, slept by night, she was abused and cursed by a shrill chorus of countless voices. Several times she was mobbed by a mass of swallows who flew at her in a steady stream. Bewildered and frustrated by their dive-bombing tactics, she shuffled off in sullen dignity.

East of Deadman Bay the sow reached the coast. She argued with some raucous gulls and took possession of the carcass of a Pribilof fur seal. An old warrior of many seasons, the bull had sickened at sea and wandered too far to the east. Infested with hookworm and doomed to die, he had crawled ashore and remained half alive while a dozen tides came and went, first washing over him and then leaving him wedged between sea-battered rocks.

The gulls had started to feed on him before he was dead. His eyes were taken first. He had lost both the will and the strength to resist, yet the power of life within him was too strong to allow an easy surrender. The natural order of things began drawing his chemistry back into the cauldron while he still lived.

The sow drove the gulls away and began to feed after ending the seal's misery with a single blow of her great paw. That night she bedded down in a clump of trees at the head of the cove and reclaimed the carcass the following morning. A hundred gulls moved among the rocks nearby and hovered overhead, maintaining their lament. Her indifference seemed to anger them further. Beyond the tide-pools more gulls floated on the momentarily gentle swells, blue, gray and white corks, animated and shrill. A pair of bald eagles perched like sentinels on a nearby tree. Despite their aloof and perhaps noble appearance they hungered for the carrion no less than the other birds.

As summer approached, the sea birds along the coast increased in numbers and variety. Summer visitors, the common snipe, rock sandpiper, mew gull, black-legged kittiwake and Arctic tern, added their endless movement and noise to those of the permanent shore residents, the glaucous-winged and herring gulls. The magnificent golden eagle, a summer visitor only, appeared and matched aerobatics with the bald eagle who was king year-round. Loons, grebes, albatrosses, shear-waters, petrels, cormorants, geese, ducks, whistling swans, sandhill cranes, murrelets, puffins, scoters, oyster-catchers, some resident, some purposefully present, some transient, and others accidental, appeared by the thousands and turned the great Island into a vast aviary. Short-tailed weasels and red foxes worked their way along ledges and into brush piles to harry the ground nesters, and destroyed thousands of eggs and fledglings. The Island feasted on its own abundance. A billion times a billion food chains took microscopic form in the soil and the sea. On land the great bear was the largest creature and in the sea it was the whale, but each depended, ultimately, on animals too small to be seen by the naked eye to supply the chemicals upon which the whole complex scheme of life was based.

Miles at sea millions of salmon were bursting with their own fertility, and in an ancient and mysterious way were homing in on the network of rivers and streams from which they had originally come.

Through this panorama the sow trudged her steady way. Fearing only the scent or sound of man, unafraid of any other living thing and without the capacity to fear what did not live, she moved, a great, furred hulk. Nothing deterred her, nothing could resist her. She feasted endlessly on plant life, on animal life she took, and on occasional carrion. Her eating was with a purpose as profound as her mating. By late fall, because she had bred that year and would den early, she would find herself a cave and survive off the spring and summer harvest. More than that, she would produce two new lives and feed them throughout the winter. She would not feed herself from late October of one year until mid-

May of the next. Her immense size demanded of her that she feed almost continuously throughout this spring and summer. It was all part of the same complex scheme. For nature, now, she was not one life, but three.

The lives and problems of the other creatures whose paths she crossed and recrossed were as profound as her own. Somehow, though, there was a kind of shrill panic to their ways that was absent from hers. She was more deliberate. Prey to no animal, omnivorous, mountainous in size, she pressed on, feeding, resting, and feeding again. The only sign she made to reveal that she was not totally in command of the land was her regular sampling of the air currents that flowed and swirled among the coastal confusion of rocks and trees. On several occasions she caught a disturbing scent and dissolved into the thick cover that was always near at hand. This alarm at the sign of man was the only suggestion of her vulnerability.

Although there are countless places on Kodiak Island where you can stand and neither see nor hear the ocean, it is a land of the sea. The Island's weather and therefore its plant and animal life are all products of the Pacific. Neither the land itself nor any creature that lives on it is free of these influences for a single moment from birth to death. All that is good about the land is a gift from the sea, although in some far-distant future the debt will be collected. When Kodiak Island finally dies it will be beneath rolling waves.

The bronze sow's greatest bounty that season came as a gift from the sea. In March of that year six thousand gray whales left Magdalena Bay off Baja California and began their seven-thousand-mile trip to their summer feeding grounds off the coast of Siberia. These great beasts had spent two months in the shallow water of their breeding grounds, after three months of travel, and now turned about for three more months in the open sea and four months of rich harvest in the Siberian coastal waters. They made the fourteen-thousand-mile round trip each year. Among them was a cow of immense size. She was more than forty-five feet long and weighed seventy-five thousand pounds. Her great flukes, twelve feet across, drove her northward with the herd. In April they massed on the west side of Washington's Olympic Peninsula and moved off toward the west. In a matter of hours the entire herd squeezed through the narrow two-mile passage between Salander Island and Cape Cook on the northwest tip of Vancouver Island. Then they disappeared from human view, fanning out across the Pacific to reassemble close to Siberia. Their diet of euphausia, a small pelagic shrimp, and bottom-living shrimplike animals, the amphipods, would hardly seem substantial enough to support such tremendous creatures, yet these tiny organisms are provided in such astronomical quantities that whales can thrive when free of man's interference.

In mid-May the great cow whale passed thirty miles south of Kodiak Island. Although she spent eighty-five percent of her time submerged, she was forced to come up for air in one of two distinctly different rhythms. She would dive to a depth of four hundred feet and in eight minutes cover two thousand feet of her journey before surfacing to exchange the gases in her lungs. In a more exuberant mood she would travel a thousand feet in four minutes at a depth of only a hundred feet before surfacing two or three times in quick succession. She varied her rhythm to suit her mood and so progressed away from the American continent.

With her was her seventeen-foot, three-thousand-pound calf. It had been born in February and like all young whales had been extremely precocious. It swam immediately following its birth and had been able to rise to the surface for its first breath unaided. It now stayed close to its mother as they moved westward.

To the west of Kodiak Island the cow submerged on one of her long, deep dives and for reasons that cannot be understood failed to detect a ship that was heading northward toward the Shelikof Strait. Moments after she surfaced the collision took place. The ship shuddered and stopped. The wounded whale sank immediately and then slowly rose, blood pouring from the deep gashes which the ship's screws had slashed into her back and side. Sick, disoriented, she circled aimlessly, blowing at one-minute intervals. She could not fill her lungs and remain close to the surface.

With her confused and terrified calf near her, the cow drifted slowly toward the east and came to the southern shores of Kodiak Island. Several times she attempted to reorient herself to her normal migratory route but she was too badly hurt to function properly.

The blood that continued to seep into the sea acted as

a homing device for other animals. On the second day of her agony fourteen six-foot-tall fins cleaved the greasy swells a few thousand yards offshore and a pack of killer whales struck. The calf was quickly taken, cut in half in two bites and soon the cow herself was dead. Her carcass, with perhaps twenty thousand pounds of flesh missing, floated ashore in a cove not far from where the fur seal had died. The bronze sow came upon it a few hours later.

Again, the contest with the gulls began. The cove came alive with noise and movement as crows and magpies joined in the orgy. Foxes moved with exaggerated stealth in sheltered spots, and the sow feasted. A young boar, whose nose had easily detected the stench that grew in potency by the hour, edged along the shore and came to within a hundred feet of where the sow sat hunched over a morsel she had torn loose. She rose cautiously and took two awkward steps forward on her hind legs. Sniffing, sampling, she soon found the boar and dropped on all fours, chopped her jaws together, roared and charged. The young male, much too small to accept such a challenge, vanished into the thick cover whose side he had never left. She pulled up and stood leaning slightly forward against the wind. A swirl of air destroyed the trail and she did not press the attack. When she returned to her meal she found a blanket of birds covering it and two foxes tugging frantically at the morsel she had taken for herself. Again she charged with a violently explosive roar, sending birds and foxes scurrying for safety. Several gulls had eaten too much and were struggling to get off the ground. One of these she killed with a casual flick of her paw. As she settled back to her feeding, a fox, cheated of his prize, snatched the dead gull instead and dragged it off into the brush.

Here at the edge, where land and sea had indistinct boundaries, life blended and shared a common bounty. Bits and pieces of whale flesh drifted out with each tide and scavenger fish gathered at the surface to feast, just as their counterparts on land took advantage of the same situation. Only an occasional flare of bad temper made the sow notice any of this. Once, when the tide brought the water around her feet, she began dancing in the rising sea, slapping at the fish who had moved in with their element. She quickly circled the whale, slapping at the Dolly Varden, the char known to most as a trout. This large and active fish, most carnivorous of the Salmonidae, was named by persons unknown for the gay and enchanting girl in Charles Dickens's *Barnaby Rudge*. Now, schooling around the whale, the char infuriated the sow. She killed one giant of nearly twenty pounds, shook it in her jaws, then dropped it. It drifted ashore where two foxes were waiting to claim it before the gulls, who were now overhead in the thousands. Again two bald eagles posted themselves in a tree near the arena too proud, or perhaps too shy, to join in the uproar. They would wait for a quieter time to claim their share.

Eventually the tide rose too high for the sow and she had to relinquish her prize to the fish for a few hours. Her temper was as sodden as her fur when she waded ashore, and the young male bear could consider himself fortunate that he had not encountered her in this mood. The appearance of the gray whale carcass had arrested the movement of the sow toward the west, and by the time a huge boar appeared a week after the whale had drifted ashore and drove her off, the sow had become more or less fixed in the area. In the summer weeks remaining she would work some berry patches on higher ground nearby, and the salmon streams would get her careful attention. When October rolled over the land she was still in the region and had found her den site. It was here, near Deadman Bay, that her cubs would be born. Their birthplace had in part been determined by an accident that occurred at sea between a whale from the waters of Mexico bound for the waters of Siberia, and a freighter of Japanese registry.

 3.

SELECTING THE HIGHEST GROUND SHE COULD FIND, THE
sow forced her way through some bushy debris that
blocked the entrance to a rock tunnel running a dozen
feet into the hill. The natural cave had the preferred
southern exposure and she set about lining the floor
at the far end. She managed to accumulate a fair pile of
alder branches and mosses and, sweeping with her amaz-
ingly dexterous paws, spread them about until the floor
was covered to a depth of a foot. This was a refine-

ment some bears do not bother with. As if to sample her work she entered the den several times during the first few days and slept for two or three hours at a stretch. After these short naps she would emerge and feed on whatever was at hand.

The cave site was on a prominence 2,851 feet above sea level behind Alpine Cove at the northeast end of Deadman Bay, which is itself an extension of Alitak Bay. There was little to be had on the higher portions of the slope and the sow worked her way down to feed. She stopped from time to time to nose along grass tunnels in open areas and gulp down the diminutive tundra voles she found.

In a general mopping-up operation she ate whatever she could find — dead grass, high-bush cranberries, a few old salmon carcasses found beside a stream, a few blueberries that had survived the late summer. She found the lost or abandoned jacket of a hunter and worried it for several minutes. She finished by eating bits and pieces of it. The fact that it reeked of man-smell yet was inanimate seemed to please her. Her almost puppy-like postures as she tossed it about and pounced on it were ludicrous because of her great size. It is such unexpected behavior as this that has earned bears an altogether unsuitable reputation as natural clowns.

Twenty-six years earlier, in 1924, a small herd of Sitka black-tailed deer had been transported to the Island by men seeking to establish new sport, and although most of the descendants of these imports now lived to the northeast, a few had wandered toward the west. One of these, a prime buck, had been shot at earlier in the year by an amateur hunter and had stumbled off into a thicket to die in agony. The sow came upon the rotting carcass and found it just to her liking. Had she made the kill herself she would have eaten very little before burying it and waiting for it to putrefy. Her crushing-type premolars and molars were better able to handle flesh that had been dead for some time, and the higher the flesh the better she liked it.

The good fortune the sow had realized in finding first a bull fur seal, then a gray whale, and lastly the buck, in addition to her normal quota of salmon and small game, had given her more animal food in one year than she had consumed in the previous three combined.

The last food she consumed before finally retiring consisted of a few frozen berries and then, one very rainy, cold afternoon, she disappeared into her den for nearly half a year of sleep.

It took her some time to settle down and she lay awake for many hours, listening. She was unlikely to be disturbed but still she listened, her nerves strangely taut. Quite aside from the fact that she had laid claim to the cave, this was a nursery. Without any real understanding of the situation, she sensed that she must defend this place. The chemical changes within her body were releasing behavioral patterns, and she would be held prisoner by them for months to come. She could not reason them out, but she could and did respond to them.

In terms of human knowledge and understanding, the

whole matter of territorialism among bears is a perfect muddle. Bears, whose behavior is contradictory at best, have kept this secret well. They *appear* to be more concerned with the specifics of life than with abstracts like territory. If there are cubs, a sow is likely to defend them; if a male has a mate, he is likely to drive off other males. Similarly, if there is a food cache or a preferred fishing spot along a stream, the largest and strongest animal is likely to prevail in any dispute. But whether or not a bear actually establishes a territory is open to question and, on some evidence at least, even doubtful. The so-called "bear tree," a well-clawed tree often described as a territory boundary marker, may have other meanings entirely. We do not know.

This cave behind Deadman Bay, however, was a specific, and the sow would not allow another bear to share it with her. Her temper, short at all times, would be even worse when her winter sleep was upon her. Perhaps unwittingly, she had left enough of her signs around to warn off any intruder. Only a fool would ignore them.

As the sow slipped slowly off to sleep, forces in nature were transforming the Island. The steadily declining temperature was causing minute changes that would continue to accumulate until the land, its lakes, and its streams were no longer recognizable. These changes, although microscopic at first, carried the insistence of universal laws. Their chemistry and their physics were basic to the nature of matter itself and as open to influence as the orbits of planets and the forward surge of time. The fresh water that had flowed so freely throughout the spring, summer and early fall was changing form. As a liquid it consisted mostly of dihydrol molecules. As it slipped downward, away from the boiling point it had never approached even on the hottest day, the percentage of *tri*hydrol molecules increased. On the third day of the sow's sleep the temperature reached 32 degrees Fahrenheit and heat flow out of the water was sufficient to allow a trihydrol saturation to occur. Ice appeared, first as a colloid, without crystalline form. Small disklike particles formed and then began to congeal. Soon it was visible to the naked eye. In the quieter waters on the Island it was feathery and light. In the more agitated streams, broken spicules marked the transformation. On the fourth day, only the fastest flowing streams remained uncoated and even in these the ground gru or bottom-forming ice appeared. The new ice on the quieter ponds, the lolly ice, was without the buoyancy it would have later. It was still highly plastic but hardened hour by hour. The fog rolling in from the relatively milder sea began to freeze and soon every blade of dead grass, every branch on every tree was covered with rime. Rain fell and turned to sleet. And still the temperature fell. The sky was ashen and the sun was a pale yellow disk in the sky.

The weasels and the foxes, the wintering birds, and all of the other life on the Island that had been ordered by nature to face the winter awake and exposed to its dangers, huddled in whatever cover was available. Their winter coats had grown over the preceding weeks but it would take days for them to acclimate to the sudden change. In time, atmospheric water vapor precipitated out and fell as billions of hexagonal crystals. Although each was a masterpiece of sculpture, a thing of unparalleled beauty, no one appreciated the fact. All eyes, human and animal alike, were focused on grosser facts. The land was white again and winter had retaken Kodiak Island.

Cold air flowed steadily across the warmer waters in the harbors and bays that indented the coast. Weird frost smoke drifted across peninsulas and changed the once green and vital shores to mysterious etchings. Rocks and trees drifted in and out of the freezing fog like ghost ships. The difference between night and day seemed less well defined. Winds blew down from the north and compacted the snow. By the end of the first week the smaller animals could walk across the wind-crust without breaking through. As the bretts formed under the incessant hammering, ever larger animals would be able to do the same. This packed snow meant, though, that foraging became more difficult. In these first weeks of winter a selection would be made. Many wintering animals that were old, past their prime, would die. The young born that spring and summer that were not fit to live and breed the following year would also be lost. The toll mounted and the carrion eaters rejoiced in the new bounty. But their good fortune was of brief duration, and many of them were soon in trouble as well. Having created blindly, having created too much, nature had come full circle to the time of culling.

Inside of her cave the sow was oblivious to the transformations taking place in the land, killing animals by the hundreds. Her great body, luxurious in its winter coat and insulated with fat, moved rhythmically in her sleep. She was not hibernating, for she did not have that strange power. The ground squirrels *were* hibernating, their respiration, temperature, and heart rate reduced almost to the point of death. But the sow slept, her vital processes nearly normal. If disturbed, she could awake and, although it would take her some minutes to collect herself, she would be quick enough to meet any threat, real or imagined. The rodents, sleeping in deeper places, could not do this. The two phenomena — hibernation and winter sleep — are quite different.

On two occasions during the long winter months the sow would wake and shuffle out of her den in an almost drunken stupor. Finding nothing to eat and not quite understanding what she was doing out in the cold in the first place, she would return to her den. Her tracks, for no snow crust could bear her weight, would soon be filled in by fresh snowfalls and wind-driven diamond dust, incredibly fine flakes no more than five one-thousandths of an inch wide. Inside her den her huge body, acting like a radiator, would soon raise the temperature again to a comfortable level and her snoring would attest to her comfort and security. There are decided advantages to being the largest animal in the land.

Outside, the wind and the cold continued and the transformation of the world progressed. Snow that had fallen as cottony flakes, huge aggregates of tiny crystals, began to firnicate and lose its form. Snow, like everything else, must age and firn snow, or névé, replaced the fresher falls. The winter fix was complete. Only the hardiest, and those able to sleep, could survive. The cold itself was more than a measurement on a thermometer. It was a vital force that maimed and killed.

Once she had fallen asleep the sow's body accelerated the business of creation. Embryonic growth was rapid, for a new timetable had to be met. Within her, two cubs grew. Protected from the harsh reality of the winter world, and even from the relative warmth and calm of the cave, their tiny bodies were nourished by the store the sow had instinctively provided. By early December their bodies were each about one fifteen-thousandth the weight of their mother. If they were to survive their birth they would have to increase that weight tenfold in eight or nine weeks. This, their first challenge, was an unconscious one. Deeply implanted in the magic chemicals, they grew, were nurtured, guarded, truly created in a repetition of the most ancient and marvelous miracle of all.

On the last day of January, the sow gave birth. Her two cubs each weighed eleven ounces. Blind, toothless, hairless, the cubs could not survive without the protection of their mother's body. She curled around them, approximating a pouch with the rolls of fat that girded her, and slept again as they began to suckle. For at least nine months and perhaps much longer, she would feed them from her own body. The fact that the cubs had been born was a significant change in status, to be sure. It required of her different chemical processes. In the longer view, however, the change was almost academic. She was no more or less the provider now than before. Her life was their life and her death would be followed in hours by theirs.

At the end of forty days the cubs' eyes were open and they had cut their first teeth. Although more active each day, and more demanding, they seldom moved more than inches away from the great fount of warmth and nourishment. Their bodies were furred now and there was a measure of coordination in their movements. But had the mother moved away from them for even a few minutes they would have panicked and whined piteously.

No one can know how many hours the sow slept and how many she lay awake, caressing, cleaning and generally attending to her cubs. She was almost unbelievably gentle with them and tolerant of their increasingly bad manners. Her own vent was stopped with a resinous plug and the den remained surprisingly clean. The bear stench was unmistakable, though, and her own particular smell was so firmly implanted in the senses of the cubs that they would not forget it until chased away by her more than a year later. For the two cubs, the male and the female, the world was dark, soft and rich in smell. The only thing that changed was themselves. Everything else was a reassuring constant.

Winter passed, finally, and a satisfying richness returned to the land. The animals that had survived began to move with a new freedom and there were fresh crops to harvest everywhere. The table was reset and the feast began again.

April came, unlocking a land long gripped in severe winter conditions. Yet the sow did not emerge. Her cubs were by now truly playful and she slowly began to exert the first slight pressure of her authority. By the time she brought her cubs out into the open, in mid-May, they would weigh fifteen pounds and be far too active for her to allow them a free hand. Immediate response to her demands was a prerequisite to their survival. The dangers for the young, even the young of giants, are very real. The grumpy males would be about and the flesh of a newly emerged cub is sweet. If the cub is poorly trained, it can be easy prey. This the sow knew instinctively, as she knew everything, and against this she protected her young with the evenly applied rudiments of education. By mid-May they would know the meaning of a grunt or woof and would know well the sting of a ponderous paw on the rump.

And so nature's will was done. A new generation had been born, soon to emerge into a world freshly culled and newly seeded. The sow had made a down payment on her debt, a debt that could be discharged only when her own body was no longer productive. For the moment, however, she had a task to perform. The lives she had created within her body and had nurtured in the den needed to be readied until they could be set free to incur, in their turn, the same indebtedness. Nature works only in cycles. There are no straight lines. The forward movement is provided by time. Everything within it must revolve.

4.

THE WORLD OF CHANGE INTO WHICH THE CUBS EMERGED
was already far advanced. Cubs of previous seasons, the
yearlings, sows that had not bred the summer before,
and the unpredictable males were about. The influx of
bird life and the offshore flow of marine mammals heading for the newly liberated Arctic Ocean pastures were
in progress. Rain was a daily and sometimes hourly occurrence and the ground underfoot was mushy. Spring
was unmistakable on all sides and summer was on the
way. Her advance scouts were everywhere.

Shortly after leaving the cave, ahead of her cubs and extremely alert to the possible appearance of a mature bear, the sow began to eat cathartic grasses and herbs and quickly voided the black, resinous plug that had blocked her intestinal passage. Her feet were tender from the long period of inactivity and she limped slightly. During the first days she stayed close to her den, eating what she could find on the higher slope. Not at all unlike a cow, she would take a mouthful of grass and crop it by a slightly abrupt lift of her head. She was still fat but would lose weight rapidly during the first two weeks. Following that she would again begin to lay on fat against the needs of her coming sleep.

This concentration on food is typical of bears. The demands increase as spring progresses into summer and the sow, never a fastidious eater, took whatever she could find. While she might consume surprisingly little for so large an animal at any one feeding, her meals were so frequent as to be almost continuous. The total volume of food consumed was larger than might be suspected by the casual observer.

Seeking the tender pooshka, or wild parsnip, the sow would grasp a mouthful of vegetation and plant her front paws firmly on the ground. With a convulsive movement she would thrust backward with her body until a clump of sod tore loose. Turning it over with her paw she freed the roots, up to a half inch or more in diameter, and slowly ate them. In her quest for these tender morsels, and for grubs and beetles as well, she turned over whole areas of the hillside until it looked as if it had been plowed by a drunken farmer. Food-getting for a bear is more a matter of drudgery than of reliance on keen senses. Having given the bear a varied appetite, having delivered it from the agony other predators know when game is short, nature has either taken back or denied altogether the razor-edge alertness that wolves, weasels, and cats must have to survive.

At regular intervals the sow returned to her cubs, for their feeding demands were no less insistent than hers. Unlike their mother, however, they could accomplish nothing on their own.

Often, as she worked the fields close to the mouth of the cave, she would leave her cubs at its entrance, but she was never out of range and she constantly tested the wind for signs of danger. When she came to them they whined eagerly and climbed over each other to get at her. She would sometimes lie on her side and watch them feed, making the softest of satisfied sounds. At other times she would lie on her back and move her hind legs rhythmically as they tugged and gorged. And at yet other times she would sit square on her bottom with her back against a tree or mound and place a paw on the back of each cub. With her hind legs thrust out in front like a comical old woman she would point her nose straight up and slowly rotate her head as if to exercise a stiff neck. The cubs thrust hard with their hind feet and shuddered with satisfaction at what she gave them. Always she was tender, always alert. Her life was divided between feeding herself, and through herself her cubs, and worrying about their safety. There seemed to be no other forces, no other concerns.

The cubs grew daily. Their emergence weight of fifteen pounds would have to increase to a hundred pounds or more by mid-autumn. By the late fall of their second year they would weigh as much as four hundred pounds. A difference in weight between them would not occur until about their fourth year. For the moment, there was little to distinguish between the two. They were liver-gray in color but it was impossible to predict the tones they would finally achieve. The genes they inherited from their parents had been too confused over the preceding generations by the influx of brown bear color variation to take a predictable form. Since no survival factor had existed in any one tone before man arrived there was no particular trend. Before nature can make that miraculous adjustment man will almost certainly see to it that the bear is extinct.

As the cubs' size and strength grew and as their coordination improved the sow increased the length and duration of her excursions. Calling to them and constantly bolstering their confidence with the sounds she made, she took them further and further away from the cave. At last she began keeping them away for days and nights at a time, always bedding down before dark in the deepest cover she could find. Their demands on her never faltered and their treks were often interrupted for a feeding session. The further they moved away from their den site the more alert she became. She seldom relaxed for more than a few minutes at a time.

One afternoon as the family was edging down through a clearing between two rings of stunted alders that girded a hill, the sow stopped short and rose to her hind legs. The movement was smooth and effortless. Straining against the inadequacy of her vision she moved her head from side to side. The cubs came tumbling up against her legs and began to frolic. She issued three rapid, harsh commands and in a comic imitation of their mother they attempted to rise up to see what had caught her attention. The longer she held the position the more nervous the cubs became. They sank to all fours and moved in close against her legs. The female cub began to whine and again the sow grunted peremptorily. She was listening to the winds, and sampling their chemistry. She sensed another bear in the vicinity — and it was close by.

On the lower portion of the slope, another sow stood among the alders and stared myopically up to where the bronze female towered. Victim of a natural freak, this bear had *four* cubs huddled by her legs. This extremely rare occurrence does happen from time to time and the sows involved are generally all but overwhelmed by the ordeal. With so much more to do, with so much more to worry about, their whole attitude is one of profound bewilderment.

A small current of moving air that had begun at sea and picked its way across seaweed-covered rocks, through patches of brush and trees, was working up the slope. The energy behind it was reinforced by other currents from over the surface of the water and it flowed and rippled across the clearing. It passed the sow in the alders, snatched away her secret and eddied past the female on the slope peering down, alert but uninformed. Instantly, the bronze sow located the intruder in the valley. Her sudden head movement and grunt caused the stranger to move, and to shift her position ever so slightly. The bronze sow was able to detect the movement and determine her shadowy outline. She gave a sharp bark and lumbered two steps forward on her hind legs before dropping to all fours, facing downhill. Her cubs were already on their way up to the ridge. They bawled in terror as they ran.

With front legs stiff, each step jarring her great frame, the sow hurried down the slope.

In the alder growth the other female, too, had gone to all fours and, determining that her cubs were well concealed, started out into the open.

The two sows faced each other over a distance of a couple of dozen yards and circled slowly until they were on the same level. In a kind of displacement activity, as if to relieve the unbearable tension that had been mounting, the intruder stopped and pulled free a mouthful of grass. Jerking her head up she quartered away and stood with her head turned to the side, looking in the direction of her opponent with the grass drooping comically from the corner of her mouth. In an imitative movement the bronze sow did the same.

Then, without warning, after having given it all the thought of which she was capable, the bronze sow charged. She hurtled across the intervening yards and caught the intruder in the shoulder as she turned and half rose to bring her great forepaws into play. They slapped ineffectually as she was rolled over twice by the weight of the impact. Her reflexes had been a beat too slow and the blood flowed from an open wound where the sow had sunk her teeth.

The momentum of her charge carried the bronze sow well beyond her target and when she pulled up and whirled about to charge again she was struck by the intruder barreling down on top of her. She felt a terrible, stunning shock as a paw as large as a platter with powerful claws spread wide and angry descended with the full force of half a ton behind it. One of the bronze sow's cheeks was opened and her teeth showed through the wound. Again she charged, snapping furiously, but the intruder had already begun to retreat. She caught up with the darker female and managed to sink her teeth into her rump before she vanished into the brush. The crashing of her great body sounded as if a truck were hurtling through the growth.

The sow patrolled the edge of trees, coughing and grunting. She didn't dare enter the thicket with an opponent so aroused and with the benefit of cover. The air currents between the trees could not be trusted and her eyesight would be all but useless.

The bronze sow's two cubs and the intruder's four had witnessed the battle huddled in two groups a hundred yards apart. They would have played together had they been allowed, for they were still endowed with a social sense that enabled them to tolerate their litter mates. They would lose it in time, though, and were learning the lesson of distrust that would stay with them as long as they lived.

Both females bedded down almost immediately after

returning to their cubs. They were no more than a hundred and fifty yards apart in the two groups of alders that bounded the small clearing. Throughout the night they both remained awake, sniffing, listening for the sound of any movement. On several occasions each moved to the edge of the trees and stood facing each other, although neither could know for sure the other was there.

On the following morning the sows again spotted each other. They did not clash, although some short charges were made by each as gestures of threat. They drifted apart after a few minutes and did not see each other again for several hours, when once again they came within sensing distance of each other. Several defiant movements were made, but again there was no direct conflict.

On the morning of the third day, shortly after feeding her cubs their first meal of the morning, the bronze sow moved down to the edge of the trees. There, not more than a dozen feet away, the intruder grazed with her four cubs strung out behind her. The wind was blowing again from the sea and the scent and sound of the intruder carried clearly and unmistakably. The sow sank back on her haunches and sorted out the messages. With a wild roar, almost a scream, she burst from her cover. The four cubs scattered but one was too slow. Snatching it up in her great jaws she ended its life with a single snapping action, dropped its small body and spun again to re-enter the woods where her own cubs were wailing.

Whether or not it was immediately clear to the intruder that she had lost her smallest cub we cannot know. Her remaining three were running and tumbling down the slope in abject terror. The charge of the great bronze sow out of the brush so close at hand came with stunning impact. Only their training enabled them to break away from the paralyzing effect of the attack and get away at all.

The intruder spun around, perhaps seeing the body of her cub lying limp and oozing blood, and crashed into the brush after her opponent. Roaring, wailing, grunting, and chopping her jaws, she smashed down brush and with a gesture of wild defiance clubbed a sapling an inch and a half thick to the ground with one sweep of her forepaw. Rising to her full height, her jaws still chopping in anger, the great sow circled slowly, worrying everything in her way. In her passage she destroyed the nests of three ground-nesting birds. The yellow yokes from a dozen shattered shells seeped out and the parent birds circled overhead, bemoaning their loss. Diminutive mammals of several species fled before the onslaught and a mouse nest toppled, spilling its pink inhabitants to the ground. When the sow had passed a weasel emerged and took the little bodies before the female mouse could find them.

The furious charge of the intruder into the brush was to no avail. While she beat her way through the bushes and between the trees the bronze sow and her cubs had vanished over the ridge above and were close to a mile away when the intruder emerged grunting and coughing on the downslope side to sit wailing beside her dead cub. She left the valley that day and never returned.

As if her cruelly violent deed had reminded her of the danger that surrounded her own two cubs, the sow was unusually alert in the days that followed. She was even short-tempered with her charges and their obedience had to be ever more unquestioning to satisfy her. She cuffed them often and bit one on the flank hard enough to make it whimper for several minutes. Thoroughly cowed, it returned to her to be fed and found her forgiving.

The intruder that had come to the valley to lose her cub remained confused and miserable for days. She never quite realized that he was gone and grunted angrily several times when her commands brought only three cubs to her side. She would look for him and stand bawling when he did not appear.

The savage cruelty of this encounter cannot be overstated. There was food enough in the area for both families and the females need not have fought. The killing of the cub was senseless and indeed an unthinking man would despise a species whose behavior is seemingly so cruel. Such a man must only reflect on his own behavior, though, and think of cities bombed and the young of his own kind dead in their smashed beds and broken gardens to understand and forgive that which is savage in nature. Although it is bewildering in any species, man and animal alike, at least among bears it can be accounted for. Bears are not equipped to feel pity and cannot reflect on agony they cause another. Bears know only how to survive. They instinctively destroy what seems threatening to them and are extremely intolerant of any annoyance, however slight. They have no capacity for guilt. Man, who has that capacity, seems unable to act upon it. The most imaginative of living creatures, he is also the most cruel, and he is in no position to judge another species harshly.

 5.

THE SKY HAD BEEN A FEATURELESS GRAY FOR MORE THAN a week. Once or twice the sun had appeared briefly but its feeble light had soon faded into the gloom that accompanied the rain. There were some windless hours, and then hours when the very atmosphere seemed to be a restless, living thing. The moisture content of the air was so high that at times it was hard to tell whether or not it was raining at all. Water seemed to drift up from the land as it fell from the sky. Every leaf on every branch of every tree acted as a funnel and billions of them yielded the water they held if agitated by the slightest breeze or any passing body. Water droplets splashing against rocks seemed to disintegrate in mid-air and hang there as part of the mist. Fog was everywhere, one moment as lacy white fingers snaking along the ground and then as a sodden blanket that joined in the drenching conspiracy.

The sow and her cubs huddled in a patch of alders near the bottom of a muddy slope. Rivulets ran down to them and the ground beneath where they sat was like a sponge. It squeaked with the pressure of any movement. It had been many days since they had been dry, even for a few minutes, and they often lifted their heads upward and grunted with displeasure. Their movements were slower and although the cubs had found great sport in puddles and mud during the first day or two, it was less than enjoyable now. No birds sang and only an occasional chirp of halfhearted volume betrayed their presence in the trees and brush. This was September, month of the heaviest rains.

Throughout the summer the sow had kept her cubs clear of any real trouble. Once or twice she had signaled them to beat a less than dignified retreat when she found her family too close to a cranky old boar, but since the episode with the intruder sow, things had been relatively peaceful.

The cubs had learned much in their first summer. They knew how to obey, and therefore they had a chance to survive. They had learned that the company of their own kind was undesirable and that all other forms of life were nothing more than prospective meals. What could be caught should be caught and eaten. Although a butterfly was good to pounce on, the instinct for play was to be generally restricted to litter mates and to some extent the mother. She was less tolerant of their antics in the fall than she had been in the spring. Her own need for solitude had not yet had much real influence on her maternal drives but the rudiments of the separation that would take place the following year could already be seen in her occasionally short temper. At first everything the cubs did was acceptable. In this, their first autumn, less than everything. By May or June of the following year, all harmony would be gone and the family would split apart forever.

In a way, it might be said that what the cubs really learned was to be disagreeable. As they learned directly from the sow, the teacher, and indirectly as constant observers of her ways, they became more and more suspicious. When their family tie was finally broken they would be ready to don the true mantle of the bear. They would trust nothing, be hostile to almost everything.

The water that fell on Kodiak Island throughout the spring, summer, and fall had profound meaning for all life. Caught in depressions and holes in the ground, enriched by minerals leached from soil and decaying vegetation on its way to being soil, it was a soup. Warmed by the sun, recipient of falling forest and animal debris, churned by a dozen forces, it provided a womb for myriad life forms. Just as it was in the beginning when life first appeared, mineral-rich sun-irradiated bodies of water gave forth life in endless numbers. While it is true enough that these latter-day beginnings came from other life already there, there was a primeval character to it all.

Across the bottom of every puddle and pond, and through all accumulated waters at every depth, the protozoans spread and endlessly multiplied. At hourly intervals mere flecks of life like the amoebas constricted in the middle at a signal from an already dividing nucleus and, as the cytoplasm stretched thin, broke apart into daughter cells, minute copies of the parent which now would not die. In the simple act of breaking in two, a kind of immortality was achieved that higher organisms like men can only dream of.

While these minute creatures spread across the bottom, ingesting even tinier ciliates and bacteria by the simple process of flowing around, over and under them, the waters above them were beat into microscopic whirlpools by the more complicated but still unicellular paramecia. Whipping the water with their cilia and spinning on their own axes, engulfing and ingesting whatever prey they came upon in their blind gropings, they multiplied rapidly in the rich broths. Every small bit of decaying vegetable and animal matter was soon surrounded by dozens, hundreds, then thousands of frantically vibrating specks. Small flagellates of many colors and shapes moved through the same culture seeking other animal life small enough to engulf. Volvox, tiny colonies of protozoans, pulsed their endless way. Heliozoans or "sun animalcules," rather like the radiolarians of the sea, formed in every pond, some having tough skeletons while others were only gelatinous with a scattering of silica needles for protection. Relentless colpoda hunted the paramecia and swallowed them whole. Puffed out, with their prey dissolving within them, they pumped and vibrated away.

Freshwater sponges attached themselves to convenient anchoring places and set up oscillations that swept smaller animals and plants into the waiting gullets. Hydras, relatives of the seagoing jellyfish, acted in a similar fashion although of a more complicated structure. With their two layers of cells these animals had taken the first steps toward higher forms but still functioned like the lower creatures from which their kind arose billions of years ago.

Lurking inconspicuously under rocks and mattings of plant life, fleets of planaria or flatworms congregated wherever decay offered the promise of food. Some of them were parasitic on other life forms and sought out snails and slugs, in whose bodies they could bury themselves and survive to reproduce. Billions of roundworms, small white strings of life, abounded and enriched the stew. Hairworms, some as long as six inches, brown and sometimes black in color, dwelt there, too. Rotifers, as small as the simpler animals but infinitely more complex, reproduced themselves in a stream of a thousand shapes.

This endless train of life was repeated in every drop of water that came to rest and was duplicated generically if not specifically in all the ocean waters that touched the Island's shores. The freshwater species were approaching

the time when the temperature would drop below sub-
sistence level. At the first sign of nature's hostility they
would encyst themselves or drive down in mud and
bottom matter to await the spring. When the sun's rays
reached them again they would spring to life and start
anew that which they had been doing since before the
atmosphere of earth contained enough free oxygen to
support a single mammal, reptile, or bird. These, the
early ones, then as now, cashed in on their simplicity to
survive no matter what natural accidents befell them.

On this host of life higher animals fed. Insects, fish,
mollusks, which in turn were food for other life forms,
dined at a table always spread. Birds and bears alike
would utilize the higher forms, and fish making for the
sea in a cycle of behavior peculiar to them would carry
some of the stuff of Kodiak's ponds and streams to
distant submarine currents, deep and secret places in the
oceans. Birds migrating south to escape the coming winter would carry in their flesh fibers and strength built up
from this harvest in the Island's fresh waters. They
would carry other creatures glued to their feet and
feathers to drop off on distant shores. Kodiak Island thus
is at one with the world. It draws from the same universal force and makes the same universal contribution.
In this strange, elusively microscopic way, the sow and
her cubs huddling against the rain were at one with the
ape in Africa, the tiger in India and the boa constrictor
in a Brazilian rain forest. Unconsciously a part of it all,
they fed their way across the land preparing for yet
another winter. Just as their coats enabled them to blend

into the shadows among the trees and bushes, so their ways enabled them to blend into a universal way of life. They were part of the chemistry of the land and sea, not just one land or sea but all that exist across the surface of a highly active planet, and perhaps throughout a vast cosmos whose boundaries cannot even be imagined. In a way as physical as it is philosophical, the distant star that blinked between two rain clouds was a part of this bear and her cubs, and they were a part of it.

 6.

THE GENERAL EXODUS HAD BEGUN. FOR DOZENS OF WINGED species, millions of individual birds, Kodiak Island is a summer colony only. Early in May a few startlingly white whistling swans had arrived and, working in concert, the permanently wedded pairs had built their bulky nests of grass, moss and dead leaves. Early in July the four or five smooth, creamy white but nest-stained eggs split apart and the young appeared. Despite the formidable defense of the parents, some young were lost but enough had survived to mark the wedges of white with gray as the small flocks headed for wintering grounds. Some headed for great inland valleys in California, others across a continent to Chesapeake Bay and the Atlantic tides.

Peregrine falcons had arrived earlier in the year after epic journeys from areas deep in the heartland of the lower forty-eight states. Black pigeon hawks had arrived from Wisconsin and New Mexico, longspurs had settled in the tundra areas at the western end of the Island after traveling from Texas and Oklahoma. Swallows with parrot-green heads and purple collars had arrived from Guatemala and Honduras, gray-crowned rosy finches with a delicate pink tinge to their underparts had settled into their ground nests after trips from Utah and Colorado.

From all over the world they had come, some common, some even abundant, others only occasional, and some exceedingly rare. They had come, feasted on the Island's richness, established territories, sung their songs, built their nests, coupled, cared for their young, and now they were ready to leave. Almost arbitrarily, it would seem, nature had decided that some birds could survive the harshness of a northern winter while others could not. Those that couldn't were endowed with other gifts, the power of sustained flight over incredible distances and miraculous navigational skill.

In the running waters of the Island, smolts, young salmon a year or two old, were heading for the sea. A substance called guanine had built up on their scales, giving them a silvery sheen and masking the marks of the earlier fry and parr stages through which they had passed in the sweet waters above the bays. Now they would go to sea to return after years of wandering loaded with the future generations that play such a large part in the lives of the Island's bears.

On the hillsides, white mountain goats, only recently introduced to the Island, stood in the highest places in the east and faced the wind. Along the coasts thousands of sea lions, the bulls often weighing as much as a ton, were slipping back into the water to vanish from the area for many months. Their trips southward would be noted by fishermen along the way and many would be shot as destroyers of nets. The eternal dichotomy of nature was everywhere to be seen — change versus stability. Each living element tried to hold as a constant, a self-duplicating, annually and endlessly repetitive event while the pressure for change and improvement was equally insistent. The result was and is the miracle of evolution.

From one end of the Island to another change was apparent. The vegetation looked different, the wildlife population was reduced drastically in numbers and kinds, and the days were shorter. Perhaps the sow and her cubs noted some of these changes, perhaps all, perhaps none. To whatever signals they did react, they began the final preparation for the months of sleep that lay ahead.

Despite the fact that her cubs could now travel as fast as she and were if anything more adept at crawling into hiding places, the sow's mobility was reduced by the burden of her charges. She still nursed them although they took solid food regularly. It was her fear for their safety that caused most of her troubles. She would no longer amble over a rise into a new valley with her usual indifference. While she was still a mountain virtually impervious to threat, her cubs were not. They were still vulnerable and she was slow to move into a new area or even return to an old one without carefully checking the wind. She could not remember that earlier in the season she had killed another sow's cub, but she instinctively knew that the same fate could easily befall her own young. She seemed obsessed with a fear for their survival and her progress was correspondingly slow.

Finally, she did find a cut that seemed clear of other recent bear signs and in it she found a suitable shelter. Had she returned to the den where her cubs were born, which she was just as likely to have done, she would have found another sow with cubs already there. A battle and further loss of life might have ensued.

With the cubs always nearby and within easy commanding distance, she began to prepare the shallow cave. She was not as particular this year as she had been the previous fall and her labors were soon over. There followed a few short excursions in search of late berries and some voles that had constructed endless grass tunnels further down the slope. There were short naps in the sun when it managed to break through the clouds, and frequent retreats to the den when the rain began to fall. She was at her maximum weight and her coat was rich although not yet full. As she folded herself into the den with her cubs ahead of her she looked like part of the hill doubling in upon itself.

One afternoon early in October, after a particularly heavy rainfall, she emerged from the cave opening and, after testing the wind, grunted for her charges to follow. The wind had been flowing steadily up the slope when she first appeared and she was ignorant of what lay above her. Just as her cubs shot past her and began rolling about on the wet grass fifteen feet or so further down the slope the wind shifted. An eddy of air from above came past her and she whirled as a large, dark boar came to a stiff-legged halt facing her no more than thirty feet away. He had been sitting out the rain in a patch of brush, on the lookout for a brief meal at dusk just as she was.

She coughed three times in rapid succession, then bawled a provocative challenge. The cubs slipped up behind her and stared up the slope at the source of the scent even they could detect and interpret. They began to whine but she cut them short with an unmistakably stern command. The boar above looked down, waiting for her to make the first move. He was salivating freely and long strings of drool hung from the corners of his mouth. He stood perfectly still, though, and gave no indication of his intent. She was nearly frantic and began making short, menacing charges up the slope.

The male weighed five hundred pounds more than the sow and although he watched and listened intently he didn't seem to be particularly impressed by her belligerent behavior. In order to get her cubs back into the cave she would have to move them even closer to the boar and this she was unwilling to do. Out here in the open, at least, he would have to get past her to reach them. It would have cost him dearly to have tried.

The longer he stood there the more excited she became. She began rushing back and forth as well as up and down the slope and maintained an almost constant racket of coughs, bawling, growling and grunting. He rumbled a few times but mostly he just watched and waited. Actually, he wasn't at all sure he wanted to bother to attack the cubs. He was passing through the valley and, just having had done with the last of the salmon run, was more interested in the last berry crop than he was in more flesh. Still, he seemed fascinated with the great show she was putting on and stood his ground. There was almost a kind of spite in his remaining there. He could easily have turned and ambled the fifteen or twenty yards to the rim of the rise, allowing peace to return to the little valley, but he declined to do so. Finally, in an ultimate gesture of disdain, he sat down and yawned while the sow continued her show of frantic defiance.

After several minutes, when it became apparent to her that the boar wasn't coming down the slope after all, she began backing off, grunting her cubs on ahead. When she heard them crash into a thicket of heavy brush behind her she turned and crashed headlong after them. The boar casually scratched at a place behind his left shoulder. His nose pointed straight up. While he was in this somewhat awkward position, with his hind leg thrust forward where his claws could reach the itching spot, he caught the scent, the dreaded scent of man. Before he could turn to face the top of the rise he felt a sharp burning sensation in his flank. The syringe fired from the dart gun emptied its dose of succinylcholine chloride into his tissues. He was quickly immobilized by the drug reaching his blood. Although he could hear the men around him and felt them trussing him up he could not resist. The heavy-gauge needle with its dose of pentobarbital sodium was thrust into his stomach cavity and he slipped off into a paralyzed sleep. A heavy metal instrument was used to attach coded tags to both his ears, and after he was examined for condition of teeth, signs of disease and parasites, he was left lolling on the hillside, drugged but unharmed.

When the sow, hiding below in the brush with her cubs, had received the scent of the men and heard their voices she abandoned the valley completely and located another den three miles away.

On one of her last excursions of the year she wandered down to the shore of a small bay and, after checking the area as carefully as her senses would allow, invited her cubs out into the open rocky area that was exposed by the low tide. Half a dozen streams fed into the bay and their four-foot-deep channels were exposed for the few hours while the bay's waters were away. The cubs moved in and out of the streams and made a game of struggling up the weedy banks. She poked about nearby, gathering bits and pieces of edible flotsam stranded on the black rocks between the tufts of greenish-yellow seaweed. The cubs stopped from time to time to break the warty air sacs of the seaweed clumps between their teeth. A general picnic atmosphere prevailed.

The actions of the family were carefully watched from the bed of a stream on the far side of the flats. The intruding barrel of a ciné zoom lens poked out between the reeds on the stream's bank and panned slowly, capturing the cubs' play on color film.

Suddenly the sow stopped her feeding and looked off across the flats. The wind was from her back and she could detect no alien scents, yet she knew something was wrong. The soft whirring of the camera had reached her but could not be identified. Had she caught a scent her warning to her cubs would have been instantaneous. The sound left her only uncertain. A bear really only believes his nose.

Still, there was something wrong. She began working across the flat toward the sound. She half rose up several times and scouted the wind, but still she wasn't sure. Behind her the cubs continued their play.

She slipped down into a stream bed and was lost to the camera behind a screen of grass and reeds. The guide who had brought the photographer into the cove unlimbered his .375 Magnum and checked the chamber. He always felt uncomfortable when he lost sight of a bear, particularly a suspicious female with cubs.

Finally the sow mounted the bank of the stream and at a distance of only fifty feet went up on her hind legs. The zoom lens tilted up to catch her full size and she saw the movement. She dropped, woofed, turned and ran. She hit the streams and puddles that intervened between her and her cubs like an express train and water showered up around her in a silvery spray. She passed her cubs at a full run and without further command they fell in behind her. The cameraman was able to follow the vanishing forms for another six minutes as they climbed toward the ridge at the top of the steep rise. Three times she stopped on the way up to stare down into the cove below. She could see nothing, not even the smoke rising from the cigarettes being enjoyed by the men as they sat on the bank of the stream and discussed what they had seen. It had taken them three hours of agonizingly slow movement to get close enough to the sow and her cubs to get three minutes of usable film.

Several times in the weeks that followed she heard gunfire but the shape of the land made the source of the sounds difficult to determine. Finally, during the third week in October, when the first real frosts were being felt in the land, she and her cubs moved into the cave. It took several days for them to settle down and after she had discouraged their play with severe reprimands the family of bears abandoned the conscious world for another winter of sleep. She had done her work well. Her cubs had survived their critical first year. Only the most unusual circumstances would now keep them from achieving their own destiny as mature, reproducing bears. This would be their last denning with their mother, although to them she was still the center of their universe and it was her laws that they obeyed.

 7.

THE WINTER PASSED WITHOUT INCIDENT AND IN THE
spring the sow emerged with her cubs. She was disagreeable at first and only after several hours of casual feeding
in the sun would she tolerate them at close range. They
followed behind wherever she went and whimpered
when she turned and chopped her jaws at them.

In time, though, she reverted to her ways of the preceding summer. Once or twice she even let them try to
nurse. The attempts were unsatisfactory to them as well
as to her and the project was soon abandoned. They ate

what she ate although she made no particular effort to guide them.

Soon she left the valley and began to wander. Once or twice she showed concern for their safety and called them to her when she scented another bear, but on the whole they just tagged after her. In the higher places they ate the meadow barley, then moved down to harvest the beach rye. As May melted into June they sought the crow and salmon berries. On one occasion they came upon an area particularly well populated with ground squirrels and the sow dug out a nest, scattering several adults. The three bears pranced about, slapping at the ground in an effort to pin the elusive prey. The yearlings' efforts were fruitless and they sat by whining while the sow quickly swallowed the male she had caught. She made no effort to share her prize with them. On another occasion, when she uncovered the carcass of an owl that had died during the winter, she chased them off with a surprising show of ferocity. They soon learned not to try to feed off her skill.

As midsummer approached their role as outcasts became more and more apparent. They followed her still but at ever more discreet distances. Her temper was shorter than they had ever known it to be and her sudden outbursts were no longer reprimands. They seemed to carry a measure of real threat.

One day the sow moved into a new valley and caught the scent of a male nearby. Her reaction took them completely by surprise. Instead of warning them, of advising them what to do, she turned on them violently and drove them off. They barely escaped with their hides intact. They lay up that night in some brush on the side of a hill, hungry and frightened. They whined pitifully, but the sow didn't come to them. The next day they came upon her at the bottom of the rise, and once more she drove them off, this time catching the female and giving her flank a painful bite. Again they went without eating and whined and squealed softly through a hungry, miserable night.

On the third day they located her again, and once more attempted to join her. This time she let them come a little closer and they fed on some twisted stalk and some bearberries near where she was browsing. They followed her along a stream bank and in a shallow pool attempted to catch their own salmon. Their efforts were comical and ineffectual. They slapped at the water and snapped at the spray, but caught no fish. She waded out to shoulder depth and plunged her head in, coming up with a squirming prize in her jaws. The water was alive with fish. Char — the Dolly Varden trout — came from two directions to mix with the frantically moving salmon. From the bays the adult char had come, following the salmon to feed upon their roe while two-year-olds were migrating downstream toward salt water. The salmon themselves were so obsessed with their procreative drive that they ignored every danger. They had only days left before they would die and every fiber of their being drove them toward the final supreme act. Only the gravelly bottom of a shallow spawning stream would halt the migration.

The sow slowly ate her fill from the thirteen-pound sockeye she had caught and left the front quarter of it on the sand. The cubs drove off several gulls, then fought over the remains themselves. The sow wandered off, ignoring their brief scuffle, and didn't bother to warn them that a boar was moving out onto the sandbar behind them. By a miracle he ignored them and wandered into the stream, where he quickly pinned a ten-pound fish to the bottom. Only after he had returned to the bar did he acknowledge their presence and send them panic-stricken into the brush with a single guttural warning.

In the death of the two red salmon more than just two lives were ended. Both fish were females and their deaths included the end for six thousand eggs that would now never be laid. The predation on spawning and migrating salmon by bears has been allowed for by nature, however, and feverishly pressing hordes pushed upstream to take their places. The number of eggs that would be deposited would be astronomical, and the loss of a mere six thousand was of no account.

It was several days before the cubs caught up with their mother again. This time she was not alone and they were driven off with a savagery that came close to equaling that which she had evidenced the year before when she had killed the stranger's cub. Really frightened now, they ran off and did not attempt to follow her again. They were miserable and hungry for weeks and sometimes lay up for days at a time as if waiting for her to return. Once or twice they would cross her trail by ac-

cident but her early drive to breed again had made
orphans of them sooner than was the case with other
cubs born during the same week the year before. The
following year the sow would have new cubs with her.
If they came close to her then, she would be likely to kill
them or at least to punish them so severely as to possibly
cripple them. Their time had come. They would now
have to survive on what they had learned during their
short schooling. There would never be another teacher
in their lives and there would never again be a living
creature into whose care they could place themselves no
matter what their hunger, their fear, or their pain.

The two cubs remained together throughout their
second summer. At times their playful scrambling
showed signs of maturing into aggression but they still
needed each other more than they needed their individual solitude. The early signs of open hostility were
most apparent when food was involved.

On one occasion the female managed to pin a ground
squirrel, more by luck than by skill, and the male approached her to share the prize. She turned on him more
harshly than she had ever done before and he backed
away, grunting and whining. She finished her meal and
moved over to join him where he was sunning himself on
the side of a hill. As she came alongside and nuzzled him,
he turned abruptly and bit her sharply on the nose. She
leaped away in pain and ran off down the slope to hide
in some brush. They stayed apart for the rest of the day
but as evening began shading the land they came together and bedded down in a small wooded area. There

were no visible signs the next day to indicate that either
had any memory of the incident. There was no need for
such a memory. The wall that was slowly building up
between them was not the product of these recurring
incidents, but quite the other way around.

Throughout the summer months and into the fall the
two cubs visited the salmon streams regularly. They had
learned enough from their first few visits to know that
there were preferred fishing areas, usually where sand-
bars extended out to the edge of a channel. These areas
were the property of the larger boars and any attempt to
use them was sure to provoke a battle. They knew
enough not to court danger.

The salmon streams were busy places. The bear traffic
was constant and the pecking order inviolate. Younger
bears had nothing like the success of the older animals;
the better places belonged, of course, to animals large
enough to claim them.

Finally, early in September, the male cub managed to
catch his first fish. The stream was choked with the first
string of coho or silver salmon. After eighteen months at
sea the ten-pound fish were returning to the freshwater
streams where they had hatched. Even before reaching
the gravelly beds where the eggs would be laid, the
males were fighting among themselves, warming up to
the violent courtship that would follow. At times, the
individual fish were almost entirely free of the water as
they pushed across bars that intersected the channel. If
the channel was clogged, some fish would push overland
in their frenzied effort to get upstream. They wriggled

in wild, convulsive movements, sending up a continuous spray of water on both sides to a distance of five and even ten feet. The noise was surprising in its volume and sounded at times as if a very large animal were churning up the water. Once over the shallows the fish would drive down into the cool, deep pools beyond and rest up before pushing through the next hazard. Sometimes the fish fighting their ways through shallows were attacked by ravens who plucked out their eyes. Certain individual birds learn this game and keep at it all through the salmon season. Others of the same species never try it.

Into this world of carnage and furious activity the cubs plunged once again in an effort to catch a meal. The violent movements of the fish startled them each time they got close enough to make a catch. Sometimes their jaws would be no more than inches away, requiring only one quick bite for success, but the salmon would whip its powerful sculling tail, sending the amateur fishermen over backward or scrambling up onto the bank. They would nip at each other or tear away some vegetation in a redirected activity that helped relieve the tension that would always mount in these situations.

At first, these abortive fishing forays were more of a game than anything else. The spray, the noise, the inherent confusion of the salmon stream satisfied the mischiefmakers. But as time passed and the hungry days built up a pressure inside the rapidly growing cubs, the sporting aspect of the thing faded and a kind of earnestness crept in.

It was on one of these earnest fishing days that the

male scored his first salmon kill. The yearling pair had found a shallow riffle and scouted the area carefully from behind a screen of vegetation. Scenting no boars, no adults at all in fact, they eased onto the sandbar and peered down into the channel as the great silver fish pushed hard against each other. As a traffic jam built up, several larger specimens began easing out of the channel and set up a fountain of spray as they flapped along on their sides at the edge of the bank. Suddenly, as if the resolve was suddenly there, the male cub pounced forward, bringing both his front paws down squarely on a ten-pound specimen. He quickly thrust his nose in between his paws and clamped his now quite ample teeth down hard and caught his fish. Sinking back into a sitting position, he held his head high as the fish flopped back and forth in a convulsive but hopeless attempt to escape the brute force that was crushing the life out of it. It literally beat the cub on the head, but the young victor seemed to enjoy the struggle. With exquisite slowness he ended the salmon's life by crushing its spine. The fish fluids ran down the cub's muzzle and whetted his appetite.

As the cub walked triumphantly back up to the drier portion of the bank the female bounded after him, squealing plaintively. In fact, she was simply hungry, although it appeared as if she were celebrating his triumph.

Larger bears can eat their catches where they will but the smaller animals are safer taking their prey off to more secret places, and the male cub was making for a clump of brush when the giant boar appeared. He stood square in the trail, looming monstrously above them. Before either cub could move he was on top of them. The male felt a stunning blow on his side as the boar slapped him once. He turned slowly in an effort to get his bearings and saw the great boar ambling down the trail with his hard-won prize. There was no thought of following or challenging the theft. He had won and lost his first fish within a matter of minutes.

A noise in the brush beside the trail attracted the cub's attention and he went to investigate. His litter mate was lying on her side, desperately trying to fill her lungs. Her breathing was so labored that it terrified the male and he began to whimper, reverting easily to his cubhood vocabulary. Somehow, perhaps instinctively, he knew there was no use waiting there for his sister to rise. She never would. A single blow from the boar had caught her just right — or wrong — and had both broken her spine and driven three ribs deep into her left lung. Pink bubbles were forming at the corners of her mouth and her eyes were taking on a dull, grayish color. The male cub crashed off into the brush and headed for higher, and perhaps safer, ground. He was done with the salmon streams for that year.

Alone in a patch of man-high brush near the top of a hill the male yearling lay down and let his muzzle sink onto his paws. His litter mate was dead, his mother was no longer to be found and all other bears were his foes.

Until he was old enough to breed — until he was four years old and well on the way to the maturity he would finally realize at seven — he would remain apart.

He would bully smaller bears and avoid bigger ones. Now a full four hundred pounds in weight, he was strong enough, and wise enough, to survive. He was no longer a cub. He was a young bear facing his second full winter, his first alone. Inside he still felt very much like a cub, though. His solitude was still strange and for many weeks to come, until, in fact, he went into his winter sleep, it would be a frightening thing as well.

 8.

THE START OF THE YOUNG BOAR'S THIRD SPRING WAS NOT
unlike the two that had gone before, except that he was
now alone. He had changed during the winter and had
begun to lose his cublike appearance. These were the
last months of his adolescence. On his trip down to the
edge of the bay he crossed the paths of several other
bears and surprised himself with the sounds he made. He
had far more volume and variety than control.

It was low tide when he reached the water's edge and
he made his way out onto the slippery rocks to poke

among the overlapping strands of seaweed that formed the sleek green and yellow carpet. Although he moved cautiously he slipped several times and finally took a bad fall against a protruding rock. He stopped briefly to nurse his indignity but in a few minutes was off again.

Traveling in a half circle, he was soon again approaching the shore. Fifty feet from the high-water mark he found a seal carcass half buried in the kelp. It was very high and insects of several kinds formed an undulating cover over it. He sniffed it, poked at it, and finally turned it over with his paw. It had been a young animal and the twenty-five pounds of it that remained offered no challenge to his growing strength. At first he was indifferent to it as food, yet the smell of decaying flesh was attractive. His interest built and, as he was about to begin his meal, he sensed that he was not alone. He went back on his haunches, then up on his hind legs. Halfway out from the forest's edge, no more than twenty-five feet away, was another young boar. Although the coppery tan intruder was a cub of his year and within a dozen pounds of being his own size, the sight of the strange bear nearly paralyzed him. He was still reacting by reflex, as his mother had taught him to do. The kind of blind courage that was his heritage was not yet available to him as the automatic reaction to a challenge.

Frightened though he was, he somehow held his ground. He had an advantage over the other two-year-old that was more telling than even size would have been: he was at the carcass first. The other had had to come out from cover to challenge him. The further from cover it got, the more its courage failed. Its movements were hesitant, betraying its indecision and further bolstering the nerve of the young boar already in possession of the seal.

When they were no more than ten feet apart the cub abandoned his treasure and charged the intruder. Without a moment's hesitation the stranger turned and fled toward the trees. As it neared cover it swung around and faced its pursuer who, now far from the seal and approaching strange surroundings himself, was losing his resolve. At the first sign of a countercharge the young male turned and fled toward the trees a half mile away across the flat. As he approached the spot from which he had first emerged his courage built up and he careened off the bank and countercharged himself. The other bear was now caught in the open and far from cover that he knew, and he in turn wilted before the attack. The serious business of attack and retreat lasted for nearly half an hour. No decision was reached, for neither cub really wanted the fight that was potentially there, but the expression of will was important for each. They parted after both were exhausted and the sea reclaimed the carcass of the seal from which neither had fed.

Throughout the summer months the young male retraced many of the paths he had followed as a cub behind his mother. He realized no nostalgia and did not recognize places or things as such, yet each item in the landscape's inventory impressed itself upon him until he came to know the area in an almost instinctive kind of way. He traveled with ease and assurance and hesitated only when he caught the scent of another bear. Once or twice he was startled by the sound of planes overhead and once raced wildly through two miles of dense brush after having emerged onto an open beach of pebbles and rock rubble to be met by a sea plane taxiing up onto the beach, its twin engines roaring a terrible warning. His frantic retreat was observed by practiced eyes in the cabin of the plane that noted his size and estimated the years it would take before his stretched hide would be of interest to a hunter up from the "lower 48."

On several occasions he was spotted through binoculars from boats that moved along the coast. He was too young to attract the attention of a trophy hunter but the guides who brought the sportsmen to the area each year made note of his darkening coat and mentally added him to their informal census. He was filed away for future reference. The professional hunters whose business it is to bring their well-armed clients to the hunting areas each year can afford to wait. Theirs is a continuing trade. There is a crop for harvesting each year but it is always reassuring to know what is coming up in the future.

Although he had had little experience with mankind while he was in his mother's care the young male had been taught to shy at the distinctive man-smell. As he increased in size — he already weighed nearly five hundred pounds — the threat from other bears diminished. In his eighth year he would be a more than worthwhile trophy animal and by the time he was ten he would be a prime target and in grave danger each spring and fall. There are years when the brown bear harvest on the

Kodiak Islands reaches two hundred and every man's gun is turned on the larger boars, for these are the specimens that can make the record book. For six years more, however, he would be safe from trophy hunters. Too much time spent along the shore could be dangerous, though, for many fishermen will rest their Magnums across the gunwales and shoot at any bears spotted at distances up to three hundred yards. The fact that bears eat salmon is their excuse for this senseless slaughter.

The young boar had deepened to a chocolaty brown by the time his third winter was approaching. He had a particularly uniform coat. In the years ahead he would be easy to spot. His dished-in profile, heavy limbs and robust size and shape would not distinguish him from other bears, but the even chocolate tone of his coat would. He would be seen several times each year and would be closely identified with the area.

The salmon run that year had been late in starting, as it sometimes is, and the bears had been grumpy as they were forced to live off stream-side greenery and wait for their annual fish course. There had been a great deal of brawling along the streams and several bears had been permanently injured in scuffles that had graduated into all-out battles. The chocolate male had been lucky to avoid real injury, for he had twice encountered the lighter male with whom he had dueled briefly on the seaweed flats over the carcass of the seal. On those two occasions they had blundered into each other without time for challenge or decision. In the thick growth near a salmon stream they had met in close quarters and for a few brief seconds the fur had literally flown. At first it might have appeared that these encounters were playful rather than serious. Such was not the case. It was the beginning of a deadly serious feud. Both young males were operating in an area of some ten square miles and at several points their regular trails crossed and their rough feeding territories overlapped. They were close in size and age. They would have to compete for both food and mates in the years ahead. In these early encounters each was warning the other of the dangers inherent in contact or even proximity. There was a survival value for each in these warnings, for both would be better off without a showdown.

Late in the fall the young boar stumbled across a small party of men encamped near an area where he regularly beachcombed. The treacherously variable winds at the edge of the bay had failed to warn him in time and he nearly bumbled into their camp. Tin cans and bottles clattered on the rocks around him as he frantically sought an escape route. He was surly for hours after the surprise encounter and nearly got himself mauled by a furious sow when he gruffly challenged her cubs. He had made the potentially fatal mistake of coming upon the cubs before he was aware of the family's presence. The whole incident deepened his dread of human beings. It was a dread worth developing to its finest, sharpest point. There is no profit for the bear in a man-bear encounter, not, certainly, in the long run.

Although his skill as a hunter, browser and scavenger

was not yet fully developed, the young boar was able to
work his way through his third year with reasonable
success. He was still far too careless about exposing himself to mankind, but he had learned to avoid contact
with larger bears. Although often hungry as a result of
his lack of skill, he did manage to provide for himself
and his growth was normal. When his third full winter
sleep set in he was well past the quarter-ton mark. The
muscles under his thick coat and layers of fat were hard
and sinewy. His teeth were developed and his powerful
claws were both weapons and tools. The pressure he
could exert with his jaws when he clamped them shut
was powerful enough to break the long bones in the
largest animal he could encounter on the Island, except
for those of another and larger bear. He could crush the
skull of any prey animal with a blow from either forepaw and his speed had reached thirty miles an hour, but
only for short distances. At a more reasonable pace he
could keep moving over the roughest country for days
on end. His eyesight had developed as far as it ever
would, his hearing was keen, and his sense of smell was
keener yet. In short, the cub had become a bear. He had
done a third of his growing in his first three years. His
chances for survival had increased a hundredfold in that
third fateful year and, barring an accident of unusual
character, he would be unlikely to succumb to any
hazard before the year he emerged from his den as a
trophy animal.

 9.

THROUGH HIS FIFTH YEAR THE CHOCOLATE-BROWN BEAR
went his solitary way, a shadow amid the trees, a momentarily glimpsed movement along the beach, a force
that made the brush stir high on a slope. Seen through field
glasses, spotted from the air as charter planes scudded
their shadows in and out of valleys and cuts, watched and
tracked carefully through 10x rifle scopes, the boar was
known to guides and hunters who visited the area each
year. He led the normal life of a mighty bear and grew
year by year toward his maturity. He was rapidly ap-

proaching the time when he would breed. His taking of a sexual partner would break a solitude he had maintained since the day his litter mate died on the banks of a salmon stream.

During the spring of his sixth year, however, an event took place that was to alter the course of his life.

The small Sitka blacktail deer has become established on the Kodiak Islands. It is smaller than mainland varieties, the bucks seldom surpassing one hundred and thirty pounds, the does an even hundred. They are, nonetheless, hunted in the late summer and early fall and reportedly provide excellent steaks and roasts.

Not all men, it must be acknowledged, concern themselves with the rules of the game. To some the laws that regulate hunting are for others to observe. In Alaska, where wildlife is considered a natural resource to be harvested every year, infractions of these rules can be serious. They can lead the illegal hunter into a variety of dangers, man-made and natural.

The Sitka blacktail deer follows an annual vertical migration. When the high slopes are covered with snow, the deer stay close to the water's edge, where high winds are likely to create clear spots and expose potential browse. When times are bad the small but hardy deer resort to seaweed. As the snow clears in the spring the deer follow the snowline up the slopes, seeking the tender new growths, and normally remain on high ground until the snow begins to fall again.

Shortly after the chocolate boar awoke in his sixth spring he started down the slope toward the shore where he was accustomed to go for his annual beachcombing. Through much of his descent he was moving down through patches of snow that the sun had not yet been able to dispel.

On the afternoon before he was to leave the snow behind him for another spring and summer, a small Sitka doe was working her way up, enjoying the tender new shoots that were appearing in the thick brush growths by the millions. Her migration was leisurely and her greed for the new green food dulled her usually alert senses. She failed to see the strange predator working carefully along the ridge above her. Two steps in any direction would have put her into thick concealing cover, but she was too intent on her spring harvest.

The young sailor from the Naval Air Station near the town of Kodiak had elected to take his leave on the Island instead of availing himself of a free air trip to Seattle. He was not really a criminal, although he was intent on breaking the law. Knowing that he would be leaving the Island in August and not yet having taken advantage of the "sportsman's paradise" the Island is so often purported to be, he was using his accumulated leave time as an opportunity for a solitary hunt. He was not only breaking the laws of man, he was breaking all the rules of good sense. He was hunting alone in dangerous country with which he was not familiar. He had not consulted a guide but had hitched a ride with a fishing boat bound out from Kodiak. It wasn't until he was on his way that he learned from crew members of the fishing craft that he was woefully underarmed for the task he set for himself. By the time he was deposited on the beach near Alituk Bay he was convinced he should not seek his illegal bear with the borrowed .30-30 he was toting. Disgruntled and childishly peevish, he decided to try for a Sitka deer instead, even though the legal season was still months away.

The young seaman got his shot off and managed to wound the doe. The shot was not immediately fatal, though, and she escaped into the brush before he could locate her. He found her blood spoor and followed it until the early setting sun cast shadows too deep for him to penetrate. Likening himself to the cavemen of old, the young man struck his modest camp with the intention of finding his deer in the morning. He was determined to have a venison steak before leaving the island.

The seven-year-old chocolate bear and the nineteen-year-old sailor bedded down that night no more than a thousand yards apart. In some ways they were alike. Both were approaching maturity, both were often more reckless than wise. Two advantages lay with the bear, however, if these two young animals were to meet. The bear was at home, the sailor a stranger in a harsh and alien land. The bear had been self-sufficient for years; the sailor was only playing at the game of survival and his experience at it could be reckoned in days. Neither would knowingly seek issue with the other, not as long as the bear was not directly challenged and not as long as the young man realized he was undergunned.

The bear awoke early and began working down a steep bank where an overflowing stream had eroded a wedge out of the hill. Thick brush had grown up in the few years since the collapse had revealed naked soil and the going was slow. He came across the sailor's kill a few minutes after starting his trip down. It was wedged between the forked branches of an alder, having fallen over the rim of the cut when the gut shot it had received finally drained it dry. The bear sensed the carcass before he was actually upon it and began to grunt his approval as he neared it. Bringing his great weight into play he managed to force the alder over and retrieve the doe in his jaws. He ate his fill and was in the process of covering the remains with leaves and debris when he heard the sailor's movement in the brush below. He soon had the scent and hunkered down low to await developments. He would not abandon his treasure, not without a fight. There are times when one instinct will override another, even though the other may be dominant in most situations. For the bear, the drive to protect a food cache is often stronger than the instinct, or learned pattern, to retreat at the scent of man. It is a lesson all successful bear hunters learn early and never forget.

Bear and bear lore were not on the sailor's mind. He wanted his deer. His progress through the brush was painfully slow and much too noisy. His panting and the crackling of underbrush made his movements easy to follow, as did his muttered curses.

It was still early enough for there to be mist on the ground. The sailor's stumbling feet sent little puffs of fog ahead of him. It was damp in the woods, and even a little chilly, but the sailor was sweating from his exertions. Birds of a dozen species twittered, trilled and squeaked in alarm. He neither heard nor saw them. But the bear was well aware of their warning and knew the meaning they conveyed. He was able to follow the young man's every step. He himself never moved, but lay hunched down next to the carcass of the doe.

The sailor came crashing through the brush into the small clearing, casting about for a place to rest. Then he saw the chocolate bear. He gave a slight cry of surprise and honest fear before swinging his carbine up to his shoulder. Before he could find the trigger guard a single blow from the bear's paw smashed the rifle stock and the sailor's shoulder blade at the same time. He didn't even hear the bear's charging roar. Writhing on the ground in agony he turned and half rose, propping himself against a tree with his good arm. He was able to gasp, "Oh my God!" before the bear struck again. This time the charge was more considered, because the advantage was distinctly on the bear's side. His first physical contact with the fearful man-smell not having been disastrous, the bear gained confidence. His second charge did not carry him beyond the sailor but to him. The bloodied young man rolled on the ground, crying and pleading, but the bear was always over him. No matter which way he thrashed, the bear was there, towering, biting, slashing. He was too frightened to remember what he had often read in his adventure magazines. His only defense, if it could be considered that, was to lie absolutely still. The possum game is reportedly effective with some bears.

In a mercifully short time it was all over. The young hunter's face and scalp were missing and his ribs showed through his torn clothes.

The report to the Shore Patrol Headquarters in Kodiak that the sailor had overstayed his leave was routine. Some of his friends at the base worried openly when he was a week overdue and shortly thereafter naval personnel began circulating along the waterfront with the young man's photograph. After a hundred interviews had ended with head shaking and shrugging of shoulders, a crewman from the fishing boat that had carried the sailor westward was encountered and a search was launched by members of the Fish and Wildlife Service at the request of the base's commanding officer. It wasn't until three weeks after his death that the sailor was found. He was in very bad condition and his remains were sewn into a canvas bag and carefully brought down to where a patrol boat could pick up the grisly burden.

Neither the local newspaper, the official Navy report, nor the boy's grieving parents mentioned or thought of the young victim as hunting without a license, without a guide, or without reasonable care for the natural dangers his actions forced upon him. The young man, in the prime of his life, had been savaged by a killer. The medical report carried all too vividly the details of his condition. Nothing could have done it but a bear. Not a bear protecting his food cache against the intrusions of a stupid young man, but just a bear.

Five days after the sailor's remains had been found, a

plane left NAS Kodiak for Seattle carrying a sealed casket with a folded American flag on top. On that day, four bears were shot across the gunwales of fishing boats. The chocolate bear was not one of the victims. He had survived, not yet identified as the killer bear. That title would come to him in later years.

 10.

AT SIX THE CHOCOLATE BEAR WAS READY TO BREED. HAD his litter mate survived, she would already have been tending her cubs. Puberty comes later in males for reasons we can only assume to be logical, since the system works. In this area of animal behavior nature does not take unnecessary chances. The whole business of procreation is too vital, too close to the absolute center of things.

After his years of solitude the bear was uncertain of what he was to do but instinctively sensed that an abrupt change was about to occur in his life. An internal clock had been ticking all along, and now it began to sound the hour.

Several times he had crossed the paths of females and had tracked a few of them. There was a vague, undefined excitement in these ventures. In each case he was finally put off when he encountered the scent of another male blending with the enticing one he was following. He was not yet secure enough to challenge a mature male, at least not over such an unknown quantity as a female. A food cache, of course, would have been a different matter.

Early in June, on a warm, clear day, he entered a small clearing and was at once aware of another bear nearby. Although he automatically woofed his warning and rose to his hind legs to catch a confirming scent he found himself less alarmed than the situation would seem to have warranted. Down again on all fours he moved a few feet along the edge of the clearing, staying always within easy reach of cover. Then he stopped, woofed again, and waited. It was a disconcerting moment in an uncertain period of his life.

For some strange reason he found himself deeply interested in this bear and felt neither challenged nor threatened by it. Its peculiar magnetism stirred sensations in him he had never experienced before. He was being guided by his own miraculous chemistry which was taking over and directing other drives and patterns into their proper channels.

On the far side of the clearing a five-year-old sow was

measuring his movements by the sounds he made and the scent that drifted across to her. She recognized him as a male and waited for him to make the first move. Each uncertain, each young and inexperienced, they faced each other across the grassy expanse and grunted. The male held his ground for several minutes, swaying from side to side. When he finally began to move he did not cross the clearing but took the longer way around, still keeping close to cover and circling until only a few yards separated them. Having satisfied himself that this was indeed a situation that did not require either battle or retreat, he relieved his tension by grazing somewhat indifferently on a patch of tender grass. He kept himself facing toward the sow but did not attempt to come closer. He was caught, suspended between two contradictory commands. Avoid all other bears, and come close to this somehow special one. From her point of view, his coming as far as he did, and then just grazing, was the first step and she accepted the situation that it implied. She was soon by his side, grazing as well with her muzzle only inches from his. As simply as that, an arrangement had been made. It was an arrangement that expressed nature's total concern with these two individual animals. Together, they would replace one one-hundredth part of the brown bears that would be killed that year by trophy hunters, ranchers and fishermen on Kodiak Island.

There was no significant physical contact during the first twenty-four hours although their coats did lightly brush as they grazed in the meadow and then moved off into the woods together. On the second day they took a more marked interest in each other and neither was reluctant to express it in very real physical terms. They sat facing each other, seated on their haunches, lightly sparring. Their jabs and slaps were good-natured, though, and no tempers flared. By the end of the day the awkward young male was playing the fool and on one occasion flung himself across her back, his legs dragging on the ground on either side, as she ambled off into a thicket, undeterred by his weight. His apparent foolishness had its purpose and by their fourth morning together they were so thoroughly familiar with each other that neither found the closest physical contact at all disturbing. On that morning they joined in an exploratory but unproductive engagement. Later that afternoon they tried again and this time they were successful.

The young bears remained together for nearly five weeks. They coupled many times during that period and even began to show some dependence on each other's company. Such a union is not meant to be permanent, though, and toward the end of their time together they began to sense an alteration in their relationship. Barely more than cubs themselves, they had been brought together for a brief period of mutual tolerance for the sole purpose of creating cubs of their own. Nature had no other reason for their continued association. Even if the male would not prove to be a threat to his own offspring, he would be useless to them. He had no instincts that would guide him in their care or education, and nothing in his makeup could create a paternal attitude. With young cubs in tow the female would be by nature frantic with anxiety and would have no interest at all in her mate of the preceding season. There was nothing to do but part.

By mid-July the boar was alone again and took up a station along a familiar salmon stream. He challenged and outbluffed a particularly large sow, she giving way not out of fear of the young male but because she had cubs and hesitated to risk their lives by becoming distracted in an encounter that could be avoided. The position the bear staked for himself was on the downstream edge of a sandbar. There was a much better area beneath a waterfall a few dozen yards upstream. Here a deep pool lay sheltered under a canopy of green, and falling water of near-freezing temperature exploded into mist against rocks that thrust up from the bottom. The overhanging vegetation dripped in luxuriant growth. Whenever the sun shot rays down into this little Eden a rainbow arched across the stream near the foot of the falls. A rocky prominence, eternally wet and thick with moss, jutted out into the pool and against its edges debris gathered from the whirling waters to form an artificial but constantly reinforced shallow. It was cooler here by ten degrees than it was only a few dozen yards downstream. The fish were always thickest at the bottom of the waterfall and it was never more than a step from the carpet of green moss to the shallows where a fish could be had without effort. Here, truly, was an ideal fishing spot and here some of Kodiak Island's handsomest brown bear specimens had been photographed by men brave and hardy enough to work their way upstream when the banks were alive with fishing and napping bears.

The chocolate bear knew the prominence well but chose the more modest claim downstream. It would have been worth his life to attempt to fish there, for the spot belonged to the biggest bear on the stream. The incumbent was a pale brown tank of fifteen hundred pounds whose single blow could shatter the back of any animal alive on the Island. This same giant could pick a cow up in his mouth and walk off with it. Indeed, he had once done just that. A hunter still at his desk in San Francisco would come upon this giant later in the season and the kingly animal would not survive the fall. For the moment, however, he was alive and formidable, and no bear dared approach the rocks by the falls. The following spring two more giants, only a little smaller than the incumbent, would battle for the throne. But not the chocolate bear; he was not yet in their league.

The fishing was good this year. The waters around the Island's perimeter poured back the salmon they had kept in trust. The streams overflowed with three-foot giants whose bodies were newly accented with the passionate red flashes of salmon about to reproduce and die. The great chinook or king salmon came, running to a hundred pounds in a few rare instances, but averaging closer to twenty. Their fins were mangled and their flesh soft as they fought their way upstream with their last bit of energy. Some off-season coho or silvers appeared, the males armed and angry in preparation for their violent courtship. The handsome sockeye or bluebacks arrived, the reddest of salmon meat hidden beneath their handsome steel-blue backs. They had entered fresh water earlier in the season to begin a three-month fast. In midsummer the first of them were starting upstream. Their migration to the spawning grounds would slowly increase throughout the summer but would pick up in intensity in the fall and early winter. As the time for spawning approached, their colors changed to variable reds with a blotchy, dirty white replacing the immaculate silver-white of their underside. The upper jaw bent over into a fierce hook and both jaws became madly inflamed.

In the streams, too, were the steelheads. Actually, these were nothing more than individual rainbow trout that had chosen to go to sea and grow in size until they resembled salmon. At sea they had lost the lavender pink band that gives the species its name. As they returned to fresh water this rainbow marking had again appeared.

Millions of fish reentered Kodiak's waters that spring, summer and fall, and the bears fed like gluttons. Thirty or more fish were taken by each bear every day. The solitary bears fed from dawn until about ten in the morning and started in again around four in the afternoon. Sometimes the feasting would go on until midnight. Sows with cubs did not generally approach the streams during these peak hours for fear of harm to their young. During the heat of the day, from noon until midafternoon, while the boars were sleeping off their meals and would have no interest in cub flesh, the sows came to the waters, their young always close behind.

Long after the salmon run was over, after every salmon that forced its way upstream was dead, the bears would continue to feed off their colorful harvest. Dead salmon would float at stream side and pond edge until the last bear slipped away into his den for the winter sleep that inevitably followed the salmon orgy.

The chocolate bear was a part of all this now. He had survived by his wit, he had successfully mated and his own young would move along this same stream by May or June of the following year. Unlike most bears on the Island he had met a man and triumphed. He was one of the giants of the earth who could only be successfully challenged by another giant, or a puny man with a gun. A gun in the hand of a man is like the stinger in the tail of a scorpion.

 II.

THE TEN-OUNCE CUB THAT HAD BEEN BORN SEVEN YEARS earlier was a Kodiak brown bear from the moment of his birth, specifically a member of the species *Ursus middendorffi*. In fact, though, he had been more the promise of a future bear, for a bear is a living, thriving collection of unique behavioral patterns, not just a structure or a collection of dimensions. Those behavioral patterns grow out of two sources, behavior learned, and behavior instinctive. The instinctive elements, those parts of an individual bear's way of life that come to him locked as firmly in his genes as the structure of his skull or the pattern of his teeth, represent one of the natural world's greatest mysteries, for no man can say what an instinct really is. Nor can any man truly separate a pure instinct, if there is such a thing, from a pattern of behavior that has been learned. In fact, it is probably true that since the bear is a higher animal, most of his instincts are open-ended, little more than a potential pattern of behavior or set of responses waiting to be influenced by what is learned. Since no two bears live the same life anymore than two people do, no two bears are exactly the same. Each bear is the totally unique result of common instincts uncommonly influenced by the accidents of existence. That is why no one can predict what a bear is going to do next, or explain satisfactorily why a bear has acted as he has in the past.

At seven, the chocolate bear was eight hundred pounds of enigma living in a very private world that no man can ever penetrate, for even when man finally learns how to understand the bear he will still have to talk in generalities. Then as now each individual bear will still be a mystery, conforming to no set pattern.

The large and now very aggressive chocolate bear had argued with many other bears in the course of his young life. Along the beach, on the grassy hillsides, in the thick vegetation along the salmon streams he had encountered, warned, been warned by, and occasionally fought with a good many others. He had been bested on occasion, had emerged victorious a respectable number of times, but more often had drawn no decision. For the most part he had forgotten these incidents and although he occasionally encountered former opponents he seldom made an issue of it or attempted to renew hostilities without fresh provocation. For some reason, though, the copper male he had dueled with years before on the seaweed flats loomed as a special foe. Whenever they met, trouble was certain to ensue. When they crossed each other's trails they searched around quite purposefully for the origin of the detested scent. Whether they had met quite by coincidence that first time at a moment critical to both and had had etched in their memories a hostile and dangerous pattern, or whether their animosity grew from special seeds we cannot even guess, but they were enemies destined by the geography of the Island to meet at irregular intervals.

The mate the chocolate boar chose in his seventh summer was an experienced female his own age. An experienced animal himself, he found no blocks and their mating took place within hours after they first met on a grassy slope. She was a particularly gentle animal and followed her mate without hesitation. It was a peaceable, sensible relationship.

Their first week together was uneventful except for the fact that they joined on thirteen separate occasions. They remained quite close most of the time and each was quick to rise up and search for a scent if the other strayed. They quite purposefully avoided contact with other bears and appeared to want little more than sexual satisfaction and a good meal each day that would last from sunrise to sunset. When they weren't mating they were eating and when they were doing neither, they slept.

On the morning of the eighth day the chocolate bear and his mate were excavating a hillside in search of wild parsnips and roots when the male suddenly rose to his full height and threw his nose up. Rolling his lips into a dramatic curve he woofed sharply and quickly. He pushed forward onto all fours with a belching grunt, moved down the hill to the edge of a thicket, rose up again and repeated his warning. The female stopped her digging and watched. Several times the male went to his standing position at the edge of the thicket, again in the middle of the grassy slope, and twice on the crest of the rise as he cast about and moved back and forth in apparent alarm and confusion. Patches of warm air were moving up the slope and a few wind devils spun in the grass. The sun was hot and the direction from which the scent messages came was not easy to determine. Something nearby was alarming the male and he did more scouting than eating for the rest of the afternoon.

Shortly after sunrise the following morning the male broke off his mating prelude and repeated his behavior of the preceding afternoon. Agitated, he beat about the scrub brush, endlessly issuing his warning sounds, his anger mounting. In a violent exhibition of frustration he tore at a small tree and completely denuded it of bark. The female watched with growing concern. Her mate's mood was becoming infectious.

By the middle of the morning the chocolate bear had moved off and was sitting in a clump of brush, nursing his anger while waiting for further developments. The female was about a hundred yards away and had resumed browsing through some stunted blueberry bushes. The copper male moved slowly into the berry patch from the thick woods beyond and approached the female. Uncertain of what to do, she stood her ground and waited. He had no sooner pressed his nose into the fur on her flank when an explosive roar erupted from the other side of the clearing and her mate hurtled toward them. The female was just able to get out of the way in time as the two males collided.

The full impact of the eight-hundred-pound boar moving at nearly thirty miles an hour struck the copper male and he was thrown sideways through the blueberry bushes into a tree beyond. Recovering quickly, he was at the chocolate bear before he could recover and strike again. Both up on their hind legs, they collided, lunging for each other's throats. They were salivating freely, gnashing their teeth and roaring in a transport of primeval anger. Being momentarily unable to close so he could use his teeth, the chocolate struck out with his great forepaw, bringing it down on his opponent's muzzle. Spinning dizzily, the copper bear struck out and lost two claws and three of the pads from his right forepaw as the defender's jaws closed and his great bulk pushed backward at the same time.

In the next few minutes the intruder lost his right ear, was blinded in his left eye and had the hide on his massive forequarters torn in several places. The chocolate bear suffered a twenty-inch laceration on his chest that would take months to heal. The blueberry patch was completely destroyed. The battle ended with both males limping away sick and exhausted. The female had gone off and was digging up some edible roots. She had quickly tired of the spectacle and only glanced in the direction of the arena when a louder than usual bellow reached her imperceptibly twitching ears. She rejoined her mate toward sunset and bedded down near him after casually inspecting his wounds. The copper male, the more severely mauled of the two, had moved out of the area and was hobbling painfully through some thick brush when nightfall came. He spent most of the night licking his mangled paw. Before morning the bleeding had stopped, although his tortured left eye continued to ooze for days. The grudge that had begun when the two males were juveniles was now a full-fledged feud.

The chocolate bear was not able to breed again that season and the separation from his mate came sooner than it would otherwise have done. His movements were limited by the magnitude of his wound and he grunted pitifully whenever he was forced to negotiate difficult terrain. He avoided banks and steep cuts when he could and ate considerably more vegetable matter than he had during any summer and fall since he had been on his own. Although he was fortunate enough to find a dead cub abandoned by its mother and stumbled across an easily opened fox den, he gained less weight than in any previous year. He was constantly troubled by insects seeking to feed on his slowly closing wound and his temper was brittle. Fortunately he was not forced into any further showdowns although he was challenged several times. Instinctively he held himself in check as long as he was forced to function at a disadvantage.

Toward the end of the summer his wound had closed, although the area was still tender. The tissue surrounding the knitline was badly inflamed. He managed to catch some salmon in the early fall and drifted generally north and westward as he sought easily available food. The encounter had taken place on the lower slopes of a 2900-foot mountain to the north and east of Alpine Cove at the head of Deadman Bay. He drifted westward to the foot of Grayback Mountain, then southward onto the Moser Peninsula west of the Bay. When winter finally came he found a suitable cave on a 2100-foot mountain a few miles up from the southern tip of the Peninsula. It was an area where he had never been before but the plant life and general feel of the ground were so similar to his normal hunting range that he settled in without difficulty. The pain he was still experiencing and the general inconvenience of reduced mobility made him less concerned with his environment than he would otherwise have been on new grounds.

Few animals in this world could have survived the blow that opened the chest of the chocolate bear. It had been delivered by an animal that weighed as much as four large men. Its claws were inches long, its power like that of a jackhammer. The blow had been delivered with near-lethal accuracy, and with thoroughly murderous intent. For all the damage done, however, the bear's recuperative powers were greater. Hour by hour, day by day, carefully rationing his movements, limiting himself by cunningly avoiding broken ground, sticking to well-worn trails and realistically avoiding potentially explosive contact with other bears, the seven-year-old survived. He entered his winter den not far from the weight he would normally have achieved.

The bear that slipped slowly off to sleep in one of the mountain's secret places that November had not only been tutored by life but scarred by it. In future encounters he would keep his underparts close to the ground. He would know, too, that he had the advantage should he ever meet the copper bear again. The bear that would have stolen his mate was now marked for life with a permanent limp and only half his former vision which even at full strength had been less than adequate. Despite what had happened, the bear population would be three cubs richer the following year. Before the battle the chocolate bear had seeded a larger than normal litter.

 12.

AFTER HE AWOKE FROM HIS WINTER SLEEP, ON A WARMER than normal March 12, the chocolate bear worked his way down to the edge of the Bay to scavenge along the shore. Several days later it turned cold again and he made his way back to his den, where he lay up for another week. He emerged at the crack of dawn on the twentieth, looked about, sniffed the cool breeze and grunted his approval. He was up for the year.

His wound had healed and except for the diagonal scar that cut across his massive chest like a ribbon there was no sign that the previous year had nearly been his last. The underlying muscles that had been torn had knitted well and his movement was no longer impaired. His rolling gait was as assertive and seemingly inexorable as it had been before the battle.

On the third day he encountered a younger bear, an animal at least four hundred pounds lighter than himself, and attacked it without warning. When the terrified juvenile finally broke off the one-sided engagement and fled into the woods, his lower jaw was drooping, shattered by a single blow from the chocolate bear. This is not an uncommon injury among bears and, surprisingly, the youngster would live. If bears were less adaptable in matters of diet, such an injury would inevitably be fatal.

Any shred of tolerance the bear had ever exhibited for another living creature had vanished. He was suspicious, argumentative and almost certain to take any interference as a challenge. It was not long before other bears in the area learned to know his scent. If his scent was fresh on a trail it was a sign that the track was to be avoided. Coming up behind the bear could be fatal, for although he was now approaching half a ton he could whirl from a standstill to full attack with astonishing speed and unquestionable intent.

For several weeks the bear remained on the western side of the Bay. It was no longer strange territory and he had come to know its deeply rutted trails well. He would spend days back from the shore seeking roots and tender new growth. Then he would spend days along the shore, often wading into the icy waters and just standing there with his head held high as he sniffed the wind. Twice he was seen from the air and the comment was passed, "He may not make the books, but there's a rug and a half!"

One day he managed to take a blacktail buck. The normally fleet creature had failed to clear a windfall when he caught the bear's scent and panicked right back into him. It was over quickly with the deer writhing on the ground, his neck twisted back at an impossible angle. The last struggles were ended when the bear picked the hundred-and-twenty-pound animal up by closing his jaws on his spine and snapping him downward.

After feeding for about an hour the bear raked enough debris together to cover the carcass and bedded down nearby. His ears pricked up and he half rose when he heard strange sounds drifting up from the beach. The steady drumming sound came closer, then seemed to stop. There were other sounds that vaguely reminded him of some he had heard before but he could not identify them. Soon the drumming started again, only this time it drifted away. The motor launch pulled out into the channel and headed for the sea. The geological survey team began to set up their camp. Their program called for three weeks in the area, working from this one base.

There were members of the team who were definitely uneasy about bears. It takes a certain amount of time in the woods to get used to the idea of animals the size of trucks drifting behind the cover of the brush where they cannot be seen. *Then, of course, there was that kid from*

*the Navy Air Station a couple of years ago; and then
there was that crazy drunk that camped out in the area
to get away from his wife, all they found of him were
his scattered bones; and then there was the case.* . . .

The sounds the survey team made in preparing their
camp were varied and loud. Pots fell off boxes to clatter
on the rocks, tent pegs were driven, there were shouted
commands and advice. The general din added up to a
distinctly disturbing experience for the bear. He was
doubly tense since he was guarding a food cache. Had
the carcass of the buck not seemed to be at stake he
might have gone down sooner to investigate.

On the fourth day he fed off the last of the deer
carcass and wandered in a great semicircle until he was
approaching the campsite from the south, along the
beach. It was overcast with a sopping mist clinging to the
very air itself. He remained well back in cover and
didn't emerge into an open area of slippery rocks until
he was fifty yards from the small cluster of tents that
rested above high-water mark. The cook, emerging from
one of the tents, saw him, dropped his pans of dough,
and headed back into his canvas shelter, almost splitting
his shin on a pile of wooden boxes. By the time he
emerged again only moments later, rifle in hand, the bear
had dissolved back into the cover. The cook could "feel"
the giant's eyes peering out of the gloom for the rest of
the day. The steady drizzle intensified his apprehensive
mood.

The story of the bear that came to visit was accepted
easily by the exhausted crew as they checked back in

that night. The protestations that it had been the size of
an elephant were greeted with a few knowing smiles.
"Sure, Cooky. Maybe it was a whale!"

As the crew started out shortly after dawn the following morning they paused about a hundred feet along the
trail. A tree that had been intact when they had passed it
the preceding evening had been mutilated to a height of
nearly twelve feet. It had been stripped of all of its low
branches and the bark hung in ribbons. It looked very
much as if a very angry bear, say one the size of an
elephant, had vented its monumental anger on the first
living thing that got in its way. Inwardly, each man in
the crew imagined himself as the bear's target. There
was little comfort in the thought and they went on, a
little pensively. There was no point in going back to
warn Cooky, he was as alert and as on guard as he could
possibly be.

When the chocolate bear appeared on the second day
the cook had no trouble reaching his rifle; it was very
close at hand. Still, the bear had vanished by the time the
man looked up a second time, his finger automatically
feeling along the edge of the trigger. His story that night
was greeted with somewhat more respect than that of
the night before. It was decided that a crew member who had hunting experience would remain behind
the following day, in case the visitor came again. The
short-wave radio advised headquarters in Kodiak that
night that there was some potential trouble brewing
with a bear that was showing signs of aggressiveness.
The game ranger that got onto the radio with them ad-

vised them to take basic precautions but not to be unduly alarmed. The bear was probably curious and nothing more. *Still*, the ranger thought after he left the radio room, *if he's that big he's old enough to know to stay away. If he shows up again tomorrow maybe I'd better run over and look into it. No point starting off another season with a tragedy like with that crazy kid from the base.*

The chocolate bear did show up again on the third day. Perhaps the fact that he had encountered a human being a few years earlier and survived made him lose his carefully learned dread of the man-smell, or perhaps he had a sense of territory that we do not understand. However it was to be explained, early in the afternoon of the third day he again emerged into the opening along the beach. He took several hesitant steps in the direction of the camp with his nose high, searching the wind, and his ears twitching after every elusive sound. He barely heard the click as the rifle safety slipped over and could not identify the sound. He would another time.

It took slightly less than four pounds of pressure on the face of the trigger to rock it back. A tightly coiled spring encased in the bolt slipped free and shot forward, driving a blunt steel pin on ahead. As the pin emerged from the hole in the face of the bolt it crunched into a yielding brass alloy cup, crushing the fulminate of mercury compound against the anvil and generating enough energy to cause the sensitive explosive to ignite. The quick, sharp flame emerged into the cartridge case, a small metal tube only 2.79 inches long, and ignited the nitrocellulose that had been packed there. The explosion was instantaneous and the pressure exerted against the base of the 220 grain soft-point bullet now amounted to 54,000 pounds per square inch. In a fleeting fraction of a second, through the miracle of chemistry and some very sophisticated mechanics, four pounds of pressure output had been transformed into a massive thrust 13,500 times as great, over every exposed square inch of surface within the shell. The bullet tore loose from its seat in the neck of the cartridge, hit the lands in the barrel, expanded from the heat and pressure behind it into the grooves, and began spinning. The .300 Holland & Holland Magnum bullet spun free of the barrel at a speed of 2610 feet per second. In just under one fiftieth of a second the bullet ripped into the flesh of the bear's shoulder. It held its shape at first but quickly began to expand into a metallic mushroom when the tissue began piling up in front of it. Its rounded shape and expanding alloy tip did not permit it to puncture cleanly, or to cut a neat path. It had been designed to punish flesh, not pass through it innocuously. The bullet finally hit a rib, the fifth on the bear's left side, and careened upward. It ricocheted through the bear's flesh as if it had glanced off a rock in the open air. As it emerged beside the animal's spine and spun off with its energy only partially spent, the bear crumbled. The shock wave that shuddered through his body took him completely by surprise and his grunt and cough came before the first stab of searing pain that clamped him like a vise. Almost as quickly as he went down, he was up again and took the three steps necessary to carry him back into cover. He barely heard the ejected shell case fall onto the rocks or the sound of the bolt as it stripped another cartridge off the magazine and drove it forward into the chamber. The blow had been too sudden, too damaging, and the bear did not take up the issue. He fought frantically for cover and slipped down behind a massive windfall a few hundred feet back from the beach.

As he lay there, shifting his weight and grunting, he could hear the men arguing on the beach. In their brief dialogue the cook and the novice hunter balanced heroics against common sense, sportsmanship against survival. It was decided that there was a pronounced suicidal aspect to the idea of following the wounded giant into the thick cover where visibility was minimal. Reluctantly, yet with a sense of relief, they returned to camp.

The next day the professional hunter worked his way through the brush with extreme caution and found the pool of congealed blood where the bear had remained for several hours after being wounded. He was able to follow the blood spoor to a nearby bear trail where the footmarks, used again and again over the years, had been worn more than six inches deep. The bleeding had evidently stopped and when the trail branched, and then each branch split again, the ranger quit. The animal could not be tracked. Only if he showed himself again could his continued presence in the area be confirmed. Guides and hunters that intended to visit the area would have to be warned. A wounded bear is potential trouble.

The pain was agonizing. Massive tissue damage had occurred in the shoulder but, although the rib had been fractured where the bullet hit, no major bones were involved. Had the bullet entered the shoulder two inches lower, major damage to the skeleton would have occurred and the bear would have gotten no further than the very edge of the woods, there to await the men's approach. He would have charged his tormentors, which would have meant their death or his own. The confrontation could end in no other way.

For the second consecutive year the bear's movements were hampered by a punishing wound. It was several weeks before he passed close to the northern end of the Bay and started southward along its eastern shore. He lingered at several points for days on end. A month later, his limp somewhat reduced, he arrived back at his old hunting area. He passed through the clearing where he had battled with the copper bear and headed slowly for the salmon stream half a mile beyond. Once again his amazing recuperative powers had seen him through, but he was a wiser, more cautious, and now inordinately ferocious bear of immense size. He did not breed that year and remained apart from other bears, even along the stream when the salmon were running. He fed during the heat of the day when the other bears were asleep. Few sows dared approach, instinctively knowing that the great bear with the pronounced limp was of greater than usual danger to their cubs.

 13.

THE HUGE BOAR PASSED THE FIFTEEN-HUNDRED-POUND mark in the fall of his eleventh year. His skull was twelve inches at its widest point and over eighteen inches long. With his flesh, fur, ears and sensitive nose added, his head looked even larger. In the words of one pulp magazine writer, "it looked like a nail keg." His sheer bulk was staggering and when he emerged from between two trees, standing in a patch of ghostlike mist as he did that morning, he was a sight to make even the most experienced hunter stare in disbelief. It was as if a portion of the land itself had risen to walk on the legs of a beast.

The hunters that remained behind in camp that day were not experienced and had elected to stay behind while their guide took the third and fourth members of their party out. A second guide was due in by air that afternoon and their turn was to come the next morning. In stunned silence they stood there as the boar turned slowly, perhaps disdainfully, and sauntered off behind a screen of brush. They had examined bearskin rugs and a number of mounted bears, but nothing to equal what they had just seen. Their guide was slightly incredulous when he arrived that afternoon to be greeted by their excited descriptions of the giant, but his skepticism melted when the muddy ground between the two trees revealed the unmistakable print of a paw seventeen and a half inches long and twelve inches across the middle. If it had been found in solid rock instead of soft mud, it could have passed as the mark of a prehistoric beast.

Three bears were taken by the party in the ensuing eleven days, but the giant was not seen again. The talk of him was carried back to Kodiak, and more than one man wondered if it had been the same deep-chocolate boar that had approached the survey camp on the other side of the Bay. All four witnesses, two men from each camp, described a larger than average bear of deep brown color, and all noticed what appeared to be a large scar parting the hair on his chest. The fact that both en-counters referred to an animal that approached a camp-site by coming out into the opening also seemed to suggest one and the same animal. It is not typical bear behavior in hunting country. Not typical, at least, of mature bears.

The boar was seen twice more that year. Once again he approached a camp, but was lucky enough to get away before a gun could be leveled. Another time he was actually stalked after being observed through binoculars. On this occasion he doubled back on his own trail and passed within twenty-five feet of the hunting party, heading in the opposite direction.

Word spread in Kodiak that a giant among giants frequented the area around Deadman Bay. In time he came to be known as Monarch because of his supreme size and his seemingly casual indifference to mankind and the threat they posed. There was more than a touch of awe to the name, and more than a little respect. In their strange way, though, men planned to show their respect by slaughtering the giant. Hunters coming up to Kodiak for their $175-a-day outings heard of Monarch and told their guides that they wanted to go after him.

As with all legends, there were those who did not believe. There were those who knew the truth, however. Several times that fall, high-wing, twin-engine Grumman amphibians landed in the Bay, depositing hunting parties who had vowed to get the old giant they called Monarch. Kodiak Airways charged each hunter $63 for his round-trip charter ticket. Only a few even found tracks to support the legend they were pursuing.

There were stories told about Monarch that were just plain lies, and most of them were silly. Although no more able to climb a tree than the salmon on which he preyed, he was twice reported sitting on a high branch, staring down at the storyteller. Several times he was said to have been seen strolling along a beach, up on his hind legs. In fact, the great rolls of fat that girded his middle and contributed to his awesome weight held him more and more to his normal traveling posture. He seldom rose to his hind legs except to seek out an elusive scent, and never attempted to move about in that position. Even shifting his weight while upright was less than a graceful move and he would soon come grunting down on all fours.

Monarch was never known to visit a camp at night, or at least his tracks were never found in the morning as those of other bears occasionally were. When he did appear, he had the disconcerting habit of suddenly emerging from dense cover in daylight to watch for a moment or two before vanishing again. Any movement at all on the part of the camp's inhabitants would precipitate an abrupt departure.

Hunters, both amateurs and professionals, like to talk and a giant bear is as good a topic as any. The speculation about Monarch continued to spread. The hunters who vowed to get him justified their resolve by citing his aggressiveness. He was, after all, a bear that invaded camps and threatened human beings. The fact that the men were there in the first place with the single purpose of ending his life never entered into it. Getting Monarch, or at least talking about getting him, became the thing to do. It must be remembered that all this palaver had a real dollars and cents value. Stories of elusive giants are just what an economy needs in a region where tourism, hunting and fishing are major industries. No native of Kodiak Island discouraged the talk. Perhaps a few even helped it along with an occasional application of tincture of hyperbole.

In the middle of his twelfth year, Monarch nearly met his match. A hunter arrived from New York with better than usual qualifications. His name appeared three times in the record book of the Boone and Crockett Club, keeper of records for North American big-game hunters. He had already taken three brown bears on earlier trips, one of which, shot on the Alaskan Peninsula to the north, was well up on the list. A moose he had taken in the Yukon had an antler spread of well over seventy inches, and his record bighorn sheep had a spread of nearly two feet, with the right horn measuring nearly three and a half feet around the curve. He was known as well for his massive mountain lion taken in British Columbia, and his twelve-hundred-pound polar bear taken on a trip out from Kotzebue, Alaska.

He had heard of Monarch on more than one occasion and had decided to better his own record for an Alaskan brown. Armed with the best equipment to be had, and endowed with the patience, endurance and nerveless good sense that mark the really successful trophy hunter, this man of means took the vow. Monarch would be his, at any cost, at any expenditure of time, money and effort.

At least once a year for the twenty-three years that had passed since hunting became his passion, this man had gone afield in North America, South America, Africa and in several parts of Asia. At least twice a month during the periods when he could not go afield, he was on a rifle range edging his score up toward 100/100. Of all the hunters that had ever gone searching for Monarch, this man was the most formidable. He had gone as far as a man can go in closing the natural gap that exists between his ability and that of a wild animal. He tipped the balance slightly in his own favor with his binoculars, his spotting scope (dutifully carried by his cameraman, who went along to record his deeds) and his glass-bedded .375 Magnum capable of firing a 300 grain bullet at 3000 feet a second. This man had spent close to a quarter of a million dollars on his hobby over the years and quite understandably his skill reflected this fact. One of a vanishing breed, this skilled killer chose Monarch as his goal, the high point in his hunting career.

Everything about the man was of professional quality. His shirt was 100 percent wool and had been custom-tailored in Canada. His briar pants were faced with cow-hide, his flight cap was ventilated. His underwear was of a fishnet design for maximum comfort, and his combination climbing and field boots had been custom-made in Texas. His sheath knife came from Sweden, his pale yellow shooting glasses from Rochester. The rifle that lay across his lap as he sat glassing the opposite slope was custom-stocked, and had a silver inlay with his initials artistically etched into it. The cameraman lay on the slope slightly above him, bracing the ciné camera on a monopod, grinding the color film through at twenty-four frames a second. They were shooting the film at sound speed so that later it could be synchronized with a narration to be recorded by one of the hunter's many friends, a top television newscaster. It was to be done as a favor and the film was scheduled to be shown at three of the hunter's five clubs. It was all quality. The guide who sat about ten yeards off with his binoculars trained on the opposite slope was one of the best in all Alaska, and one of the most expensive. Big bears don't come cheap.

The hunting party kept away from the crest of the slope so that they wouldn't provide silhouettes for their quarry. Actually, a bear on the opposite slope could not have seen them, but staying below the horizon was ingrained in them as experienced hunters and they did it automatically. It was one of those things, like considering every gun loaded, that becomes a reflex in time. It was part of a ritual, the ritual of death we call trophy hunting.

The west slope on which they sat dropped away beneath their feet at a precipitous angle ending on the quarter-mile flat at the bottom of the U-shaped valley. Through the valley a meander ran, catching the sun on its glassy surface and looking like a shiny gray snake. Along the banks of the stream clumps of brush and alders grew and from these bear trails radiated up the slope opposite like branching brown ribbons. It was these trails they were watching, as well as the natural hiding places along the stream, for some sign of movement. It was a likely place for Monarch to be; at least it was the last place he had been seen. Earlier in the year his tracks had twice been found in the mud near the stream far below. During their two-hour vigil they saw two smaller bears on the slope, but neither aroused their interest. The party itself was of interest, though, to two bald eagles who were nesting in the valley. They watched from a high perch and twice rose to fly the length of the valley and back. Their concern was unnecessary. No sportsman will shoot an eagle or disturb a nest.

The sun was hot, the breeze cool as it crept around them and moved the grass in waves like the rhythm of a stiff, green ocean. The grass itself was a solid, but this yellow-green light that reflected from its millions of surfaces was liquid. Slowly lowering his binoculars, the hunter raised his left hand and made the smallest of motions. The camera behind him stopped whirring and the photographer placed the spotting scope into the extended hand. It was accepted without acknowledgment. The hunter shifted his body around until he was in the prone position and quickly focused the powerful scope on the upended root of a windfall tree.

The hunter felt the crick in his neck and rested his forehead on his arm. He could feel the sweat running down his back and chest. *I'm beginning to feel it*, he thought, *the age is showing*. During the long, hot climb he had thought several times that this would be it, his last hunt. *It's no fun anymore, not when you ache in every muscle and bone.* But there was still Monarch, and the vow to get him. There could be no turning back now that he had gone this far. He knew from experience that once he spotted the old devil none of his aches and pains would matter. He was going to ache when he got back anyway, whether he quit now or went on to the end. But he was tired, he acknowledged to himself, very, very tired.

The psychology of the hunter was a complex matter. Although he wanted to kill the bear more than he wanted anything else in the world at that moment, he loved him, without ever having seen him. He loved him for what he was, for what he made of the hunter who could take him, and for the life he lived and caused the hunter to live. In a strange way, difficult to comprehend, the hunter wished the bear no harm, yet he wanted to kill him. He respected the bear to the point of honoring him, yet he wanted to leave his carcass to rot on the valley floor as his skull and hide were packed out to the taxidermist in Seattle. The man was no easier to understand than the bear and it is impossible to catalogue that part of his behavior which had developed from lessons learned, and that part which was the result of inherited drives. In a way this coldly proficient man, this leader of other men, was like the bear. He was admirable in his stature, but dangerous to tamper with. His rifle and his extreme skill with it made him a giant too. His fierce determination to administer death without real purpose linked him to a past as remote and fog-bound as that of a bear. It would take a new science to understand him. One that might perhaps be termed psychological paleontology.

The guide whispered softly, "That could be him at

ten .o'clock. He's big enough." Off to their left, down along the stream, a bear had emerged. He stood against an upended tangle and rocked back and forth, rubbing his flank against a protruding root. In yet another learned reflex both the hunter and the guide dropped their binoculars, as the massive bear below swung his head in their direction. He couldn't see them although he looked directly at them, but the sun reflecting off polished lenses could attract his attention. As soon as the bear swung his head away the three men started inching down the slope. It was half a mile before they could reach cover and the going was slow. The bear could have looked directly at them all day without seeing them, but movement was another thing. No one can say for certain how far a bear can detect motion, particularly in the open.

By the time they reached the cover along the stream's edge the hunter ached in every part of his body. Inching a half mile down an extremely steep slope is a chore for even a very young man. Once under cover, with the stalk about to begin in earnest, the hunter felt the thrill that had brought him here and to so many other far and difficult places through the years. It was this he sought, this thrill. At the onset, the hunter relaxed. His expression changed and he felt that surge of true happiness that came to him only during these moments. This was what his life was all about. It was this feeling he had spent a fortune pursuing. It was during these moments that he felt at peace. This was the chase.

The cover along the stream was thicker than it had

seemed from above, and it was impossible to move without making noise. The guide placed his hand on the hunter's shoulder. The hunter twisted back until his ear was beside the guide's lips. "He's not going to be there when we get through this stuff. It's got to be too noisy. What's your guess?" Without hesitation the hunter pointed across the stream to the far side, to the slope they had had under observation. It was his guess that when the bear heard them he would crash back into the cover himself before heading out of the valley up one of the slopes. It didn't seem likely that a bear as experienced as Monarch would dash ahead into the open. Once he turned to enter the cover he would keep going in that direction, out the far side and up one of the well-worn bear trails that led to the ridge and safety. It was a reasonable calculation.

The three sweating men worked their way across the stream and started down along the far bank in the direction of the windfall. There was no breeze in the dense vegetation and the hunter could feel the burdensome weight of his rifle.

When they came to a break in the brush where they could see the root tangle, the bear was gone. He had broken away without their knowing it. With nothing to lose, knowing that the bear was in the open on one slope or the other and making his escape, the three men crashed through the few remaining feet of brush to their right and emerged at the bottom edge. The bear was nowhere in sight on the grassy expanse they had chosen as his likely escape route. They ran up the slope about a hundred feet, turned for a clear view of the slope on which they had been sitting, just in time to see the bear vanishing over the ridge only yards from where they had started out an hour earlier.

As the hunter lit his cigarette he noticed that his hand was shaking. It was a new experience for him, something that had been happening more and more in the office, but never before in the field. He looked at his hand for a moment, then lowered it thoughtfully to his side. With a sigh he lay down on the slope and lowered the visor over his eyes. He heard his guide sit down next to him. "What do you think?"

"I think that's a bear worth taking."

"I don't think he's very keen on being took."

 14.

AS THE THREE MEN ENTERED THE BRUSH ALONG THE
stream, a branch had been allowed to snap back and it
had hit the metal case of the 16mm movie camera. No
one had noticed the noise it made — except Monarch.
At the first metallic sound (the sounds made by metal
have few natural parallels except in the songs of some
birds) the huge boar turned and faced downstream. By
slowly rising up until his forepaws rested on the root
tangle he was able to survey the woods to his rear for
scent and sound. He caught both in time to move on a

parallel track with the advancing hunting party, but in the opposite direction. They passed within twenty feet of each other at one point. After the party had passed, Monarch turned and started up the steep slope at a lolloping gallop. Great clumps of sod were kicked loose to tumble down the slope behind him as he took the steepest incline without reducing speed. The amount of energy required to propel so large a creature up a steep slope at a speed greater than a man can demonstrate on a flat, hard surface can scarcely be imagined.

There is no possible way of knowing why the bear did not charge. He could have come to within ten or fifteen feet of the hunters without being discovered. At that range he could have struck with minimal risk to his own life. He could have cut through them like a scythe before a gun could have been leveled. But, inscrutably, Monarch decided to pass up the opportunity.

Even after he had gone over the ridge the bear kept moving. He was somewhat more awkward going downhill than up and he grunted as his legs, stiffened to check his speed, thumped into the ground. He finally reached the safety of cover on the lower half of the downslope and crashed through into the reassuring oblivion of the dense brush. There is a tropism among some smaller animals known as thigmotaxis, the desire to be touched on all sides simultaneously. It is common in the small insect-like creatures found under rocks and beneath the bark of decaying trees. There is something akin to this desire in some larger animals once they sense danger.

They are reassured by the enfolding density of deep cover. Whether it is the reduced light, the actual sensation of the vegetation touching them, or some other stimulus we do not understand, many but by no means all large animals seem most comfortable when they feel well hidden. Monarch was such an animal. Once in the woods, no longer the vulnerable target he made in the open, he cut down his speed and shuffled through the woods to the deepest place he knew. Before he had gone very far he began examining berry bushes along the way.

Back in the valley beyond the ridge, the hunter sat up and, ignoring the hand offered him by the guide, finally stood. He adjusted his cap and stared out across the valley to the slope that had been Monarch's escape route. The angle of the sun's rays made further pursuit impossible. A bear cannot be hunted in the dark.

The pace the hunting party maintained along the bank of the stream was steady but sensible. Dinner was waiting for them when they finally reached their campsite after nightfall. There was very little talk that night and by eight o'clock the last of the party had retired.

For three days following the encounter in the valley, rain fell on Kodiak Island, a driving rain that had built up its force at sea. Almost as if avenging itself against this intruder in a world of water the rain hammered the Island until rivulets ran everywhere. Even cloth sheltered from the rain could be wrung out and everything was cold and clammy to the touch. With visibility reduced to six or eight feet by rain and fog, the hunting party remained in camp. The hunter peeled apart pages in a mildewed copy of a Bret Harte collection and then switched to Ernest Thompson Seton when he tired of California miners and their hard-luck stories. From time to time he slept. Between naps he wondered once or twice why he had come to this place. He admitted to himself that the traditional joys of camp life were wasted on him. It was the killing he came for, not the communion with the Great Outdoors.

Monarch had seen a lot of rainfall in his twelve years of life. He was no longer bothered by its discomfort. He stopped occasionally to shake his head and snorted violently when he emerged from the trees along the shore to be met with a particularly violent gust of rain-drenched wind. He was several miles west of the hunting camp and was free to move in the open.

The salmon were still running in a number of streams and it was to the mouth of one of these waterways that Monarch was headed. Swollen by the rain streaming down every escape route from the hills in the interior, the stream foamed as it rolled over submerged rocks that only days before had stuck far enough out of the water to be dry. The boar lowered himself into the stream, braced himself against the current and waited. He let the salmon still struggling against the onrush of the stream swirl past. He was after bigger game and he waited, moving no more than absolutely necessary to keep his footing.

Suddenly he sprang forward and with a great splash disappeared from view. Moments later he emerged with a 243-pound female hair seal in his jaws. The powerful animal was struggling valiantly and the bear was finally forced to drop her to the rocks and pin her with his two front paws. He ended her struggles by grasping her head in his jaws and biting through her skull. It was a swift and efficient execution.

He didn't eat at first but lay down across the carcass, facing into the wind. His nose was high as he rotated his neck. Slowly he stood, rolled the seal over with his paw and opened her stomach. He ate his meal at a leisurely pace and dragged the carcass back into cover along the upper beach, off to the side of the stream. He lay up with his kill that night although he did not feed again until the following morning. His deep growl and cough sent two foxes scurrying away after they had approached, attracted by the smell. Several crows remained nearby and scolded him for his greed.

Late in the afternoon the rain finally stopped. The sky was lead-colored and there was a chill in the air that would not ease until the following spring. It was past the seasonal turning point and there were no more good days left. A steady deterioration had set in and soon there would be frost, then winter. Within days Monarch would be trying out a new den. In the meantime there was still time for feeding, late harvests to be collected. The spotted hair seal had been but one brief course.

With the temporary break in the weather, or at least

in the rain, preparations were made in the hunting camp several miles down the beach. The hunter stood in the doorway of his cabin and looked into the dripping foliage that stood a hundred yards back from the Bay. The guide passed him a steaming mug of coffee. "To-morrow morning?"

"Tomorrow morning," the hunter answered.

 15.

THE WEATHER HELD THROUGH THE NEXT MORNING, BUT by noon torrential rains again swept in from the sea, whipping the Island with fifty-mile gusts. The sea all around the coast frothed and crashing waves boiled, sending spray and fumes tumbling in as far as the tree line high on the beach. There was a sudden drop in temperature as well and a chill penetrated the bones of the hunter. Knifelike pains stabbed at his frontal sinuses, all but blinding him. Even if the weather had held through the afternoon, he would not have had his bear. The party had gone inland, to the west of the ridge over which they had watched Monarch make his escape. Monarch was still with his cache at the beach.

He ate twice more from his kill before leaving the beach for the last time. In answer to the call that was sounding throughout the land he headed inland. The last wedges of geese moved across the sky, arrows to the south. The cries of the honkers were lost in the wind and the bear never looked up. Head low, he shuffled and rolled into the vegetation and precipitated a thousand lesser rainstorms as his shaggy coat brushed against the bushes that lay over the trail.

The following day was the same. The gray morning allowed the sky to muster its forces and by early afternoon the Island was assaulted anew. The wind raised its pitch and the thudding became a moan. Again the sea boiled in anger and again the beaches took the brunt of the wind-driven fury. Monarch maintained a steady pace inland and his stops for food became less frequent. He was seeking his den.

The hunter, meanwhile, was beginning to worry seriously about his health. His shoulders ached and several times he thought he felt more pain in his left side than his right. He thought seriously of quitting, but decided to give it just one more day. This was to be his last hunt, after all, and he wanted that bear.

When the sky held past one o'clock on the next afternoon the hunter felt the first surge of hope in days. The guide was ahead of him by about a dozen yards. The land was rising sharply and the trees were thinning out.

The hunter heard the guide snap his fingers and looked up to see him beckoning him on. He was panting when he caught up but sucked his breath in when he looked down at the spot to which the guide was pointing. There was the print, as big as a platter. It was fresh, just starting to fill with ground ooze. He looked up in the direction the track was heading and saw before him a rise that made him wince. The bear was heading for high ground, perhaps to a den up in a spot already selected, or possibly to pass over the ridge into the valley beyond, away from the sea, sheltered from the wind. The ground before them rose at an angle of forty-five degrees.

Before they started up the last slope the hunter knew he should have turned back. The pain in his chest clamped him like a vise, but then it let up and he moved forward.

The wind coming up the slope slipped past the party and continued on up ahead. It was too late for the hunters to start circling so they proceeded on a straight course. Monarch caught their scent while the party was still a hundred yards to his rear and came to a halt. He coughed quietly and went up on his hind legs. He came down again and began moving in a small circle, sampling the scent as he went. As soon as he was certain of its direction he moved off to one side and began a parallel course downhill. He heard his pursuers after going about a hundred feet and stopped by a windfall to wait. They passed within twenty feet of his hiding place and he moved slowly out onto the trail behind them. He could not see them and with the wind now at his own back he was uncertain as to what to do. He crossed to the far side of the trail, assumed another parallel course and began climbing the hill. He was soon abreast of the party and was moving with astounding stealth for so large an animal. Not one of the men weighed two hundred pounds, yet each made far more noise than Monarch with his more than sixteen hundred pounds.

At one point the trail was covered with a fresh mud slide to a depth of six inches. The guide stopped to examine the undisturbed claylike mass and looked up at the hunter who stood over him, his face reflecting the pain he now felt as a steady, grinding presence.

"We've passed him by. He's even smarter than we gave him credit for. He's somewhere behind us."

As the guide stood he saw the hunter wince and heard the intake of breath in an effort to subdue the pain. He didn't like the look of the man; his skin looked gray and his eyes seemed fixed, not alert and searching. He was about to ask if he thought it wise to continue when he saw the bushes move. Reflexively he swung his rifle up. The hunter turned and looked. He tried to raise his rifle but his arms wouldn't respond. He tried a second time and his rifle slipped from his fingers and fell into the mud. For a brief moment it looked as if Monarch would charge. In that instant he filled the sky, he was all there was, and even the mountain was dwarfed. The guide pulled his own rifle in close to his shoulder for the shock of the explosion. With his eyes still fixed on the bear the hunter lurched forward, falling against the guide. Monarch and the gun roared together but the bullet spun off into the low-lying clouds, spending itself harmlessly against the rain that was just resuming.

The hunter continued to stare in the direction of the retreating bear even after he was dead.

It took thirty-six hours to bring his body down from the mountain. After two days they gave up trying to bring a plane in and a boat made the hazardous journey down the coast and into the Bay. The guide had zipped the body into a sleeping bag and all the gear was packed and waiting when the boat finally chugged into view.

Within a few days of the hunter's death Monarch found his den. The chill of the impending season was unmistakable and the pace of the land was changing to accommodate the inevitable. The great chocolate boar filled the cave. He was the largest bear on Kodiak Island, and therefore most probably the largest bear on earth. He was descended from bears whose kind had spread themselves around the world in severe northern latitudes, bears that hunted men and fought with them over caves and over food. He was a holdout, one of a few giants left. His argument with mankind was no longer over a cave or a deer carcass but over far more critical issues. His argument with man was over territory and solitude. His kind had lost that battle over hundreds of thousands of years. Monarch was not equipped to judge a battle in terms of a species or a family. Like all the bears that had gone before him, he would win or lose his own individual battles. The very fact that he had survived yet another year was a victory in itself.

The story of the hunter's death and the appearance of

the legendary bear at that precise moment spread back
across a continent. For his victory, Monarch was ac-
corded even wider and more damning notoriety.
Younger men took the oath and waited for the winter to
pass. It was inevitable that the mere mention of Monarch's name now conjured up visions more supernatural
than natural. Men no longer thought of the taking of
Monarch as a test of skill so much as luck. He had ceased
being a matter of fact and had become a figment of
fancy. In rapid succession the stories developed and
spread that he alone among bears had the vision of an
eagle, had pure white markings, was a cross between a
Kodiak bear and a polar bear, was a man-eater as well as
a man-killer, had a regular hunting range of over two
hundred square miles, had swum out and sunk a cabin
cruiser in the Bay, stood on his hind legs and roared
defiantly at planes passing overhead, crossed the mountains to visit cattle ranches where he killed at least
twenty head each night before the salmon run started,
and, perhaps most reprehensible of all, was so vicious
that he was driving all the other bears out of the region,
those at least which he hadn't already killed and eaten.
Someone even suggested that his favorite foods were
wolf and mountain lion. Very few people who heard
and believed the story even knew that neither animal is
to be found on Kodiak Island.

 16.

MONARCH HAD REACHED THE POINT WHERE NO NATURAL
inhabitant of Kodiak Island could offer a serious threat
to his safety. He had taken over the rocky prominence
by the foot of the falls and all other bears deferred to
him. The copper boar, partially crippled as a result of
his near-fatal encounter with Monarch, kept out of his
way. Although the varying fortunes of the area's pecking order allowed him a position near the top, he always
backed off when Monarch appeared.

As a younger bear Monarch had had frequent quarrels

with his peers. Now, his size and the suggestion of his wrath were enough. He no longer had to fight. His warning cough discouraged the contest.

But there are unnatural inhabitants of Kodiak Island. In 1774, Grigori Ivanovich Shelekhov came on the ship *Three Saints* in pursuit of the treasured sea otter. He baptized forty Aleuts as a prelude to enslaving them and established a colony that was to become the capital of Russian America. When Catherine of Russia sent Alexander Baranof, one of history's most determined monomaniacs, to cement her empire to the rocks of a new continent, Kodiak Island became an inhabited island in the European sense of the word. The Aleuts, the six thousand members of the Koniag tribe that inhabited the island before the Russians came, had been no threat to the bear. In a strange way they revered the great animal. Their name for him was "half-man." But the Russians brought guns along with their religion, and half-men and whole-men alike were to be hammered on the same anvil. They would never know peace again. Civilization had arrived.

For all the days of his maturity Monarch would be threatened by the unnatural inhabitants of his island home. His hide was worthless as a fur, but as a status symbol it was the foundation of a major Alaskan industry. Its kind still is. In this sportsman's paradise, a living animal is what corn is to Iowa, or wheat to Kansas — a crop to harvest. Like all of the larger mammals in Alaska, Monarch was protected not as an individual animal but as part of a crop. He could not be hunted during the breeding season, the rules governing this matter being designed to husband him just as chemical fertilizers are used to husband the soil. The mates of his various years could not be hunted when they had cubs with them. He could not be hunted without a license (the fee for a nonresident is seventy-five dollars per brown bear), and could not be hunted with a shotgun larger than a 10-bore, or with automatic weapons, shotguns that hold more than three shells, or with rim-fire cartridges. In short, Monarch was the subject of a great deal of conscientious legislation, most of it economically inspired.

On any day that he was abroad from his den between October 1 and May 31, Monarch was legal game for any man with a license. For approximately one hundred and ten days each year Monarch was regarded as little more than a moving target. The gunners who stepped up to this carnival booth, however, weren't trying to win their girls a kewpie doll. In this shooting gallery only the experienced generally participated. An Alaskan brown bear is not the first big-game animal a hunter usually tries for. Most often it is the culmination of a big-game hunting career. The men who come to Kodiak have usually been many other places first. They bring with them their guns and their skill, both large-bore. In addition, they hire guides who are even more proficient than they. These guides charge their determined clients more for each day they are afield than the average American earns in a week, including overtime. Of course, when you consider the difficulties a stranger can get into in brown bear country, the price is moderate. There have been times when the hunter in paying his guide's fee has been buying his own life.

There are few refinements in the life of a bear. As a solitary animal he is not possessed of a social sense such as that found among mountain sheep or elk. As a creature of great size and strength he lacks the cunning of a wolf or a cat. He tends to blunder into situations, to bash things down, to take what he wants by force before shuffling off in his peculiar flat-footed way. He doesn't care how he looks or how he smells and is indifferent to the good opinion of others. He just wants to feel full, not itch, and be left alone. It seems little enough to expect for a giant of venerable lineage.

Monarch did not consciously think or worry about hunters; that was beyond him. He was, though, acutely aware of the fact that the world around him held dangers that must be avoided or crushed. It wasn't an intellectual awareness, of course, but a well-groomed reflex. The two tutors in his life, his mother and the mother of all survival, experience, had taught him well. The bullet that had carved weeks of agony into his body had confirmed an earlier lesson, and the man-smell and the strange, unharmonious man-sounds were signals to him that something was amiss in his world. His curiosity about these smells and sounds never left him, though, and throughout his life he was caught in the dilemma of avoiding potential danger and the instinctive tendency all bears have to pry. Perhaps because she has denied bears the acute wit of swifter predators and made of him something of a drudge, nature has equipped the bear with an almost irresistible desire to investigate. It probably helps him to find new sources of food and to survive on a diet that would not sustain other predators. It was this curiosity, this drive to explore all phenomena natural and unnatural around him that had led the great chocolate boar near to human encampments.

Every man that Monarch had ever encountered had taught him something. As a rule, man doesn't like to admit it, but he is an animal with reaction patterns as nearly consistent in many situations as those of a bear. A hunter in the field is responding to a highly stylized pattern of behavior and for an animal whose well-being depends on judging the movements and intent of other species, these patterns are discernible.

Monarch had learned that the bearers of the man-smell and the makers of strange noises generally move in a line in deep cover insofar as the pattern of the cover will allow. A man also tends to concentrate on the direction of his travel and once on a trail will seldom turn to look behind him or to strike off at an angle unless prompted to do so. Monarch, like a great many bears, learned in time that to leave a trail and circle back was the best way to handle a situation involving man. With increasing frequency he watched hunters push ahead in pursuit of the bear that was behind them before taking off in another direction they could never determine. More often than not, the taking of a bear is dependent on chance encounters rather than on skillful tracking or a real understanding of the ways of the quarry.

It was probably Monarch's reflex-like memory of the pain he had experienced at the edge of the camp on the western side of the Bay that kept him from charging his pursuers on the several occasions when it would have been easy to do so. He still bridled at the first scent or sound of man and it could only be a matter of time before the unfortunate juxtaposition of factors that had taken the life of the young sailor would occur again. Men came too often to Monarch's home range and too often crossed his trail for the tragedy not to be repeated. The fact that this danger does exist has enabled a great many hunters to justify their sport. It has also cost a number of them their lives.

There is a great fondness for the word *provocation* among men who talk about animals. Unless an animal is interrupted at his meal, aroused from his sleep, interrupted with his mate, encountered with young, or wounded, he is generally not thought of as being provoked. In fact, though, many bears, and Monarch must be counted among these, are permanently provoked. They object to the smell of man, they object to his intrusion on their privacy, and they object to the pain a non-fatal injury causes. By the time he had reached his maximum growth and was of maximum interest to trophy hunters, Monarch had been provided with all the provocation he would ever need. Man was his enemy, and although a native wisdom restrained him and guided him in the avoidance of unnecessary encounters, Monarch was a dangerous animal, and the threshold that separated peaceful avoidance and the magnificence of his full fury was low and perilously unreliable.

 17.

THE HUNTER WAS NOT AFTER MONARCH, SPECIFICALLY. His largest bear to date had been a four-hundred-and-seventy-pound black bear taken two years earlier west of the White Salmon River in Klickitat County, Washington. His wish now was for a brown bear, one with the magic name of Kodiak attached to it, and it didn't have to make the record book. Any bear from Kodiak Island was enough of a status symbol for him. He had heard of Monarch, and of the experts who had gone after him, but no such grandiose idea occurred to this essentially realistic young man. He had quit smoking and had cut himself down to one beer a day in order to pitch enough quarters and half dollars into the jar on his dresser to afford this trip. He would leave the record book to the millionaires for whom it was intended. He wanted his deeds judged by his friends, not posterity.

The guide had been reluctant to accept the reservation at first. One week is not enough to guarantee a reasonable trophy but there had been something so earnest about the young man's letter that he had made an effort to accommodate the application. As a workingman himself he could understand that not everyone who wanted to hunt on Kodiak Island had unlimited resources. He could appreciate the strain even a week would put on the average man's budget. He took the young man afield, and was glad that he did. He was thoroughly likable even if a little too eager. He would require careful watching. He could be the kind who might panic in a tight situation. A good guide is as critical in the appraisal of his client as he is of their quarry. Such evaluation is often essential if the guide is to preserve the life of the one intent on taking the life of the other.

Because the young man's time was short and because he was so anxious to get his bear, it was decided not to return to the beach camp each night. Instead they would head inland and circle around for the week, or for as long as it took to find and kill a worthy trophy animal. They had had good weather in their first two days and had seen plenty of bear sign, and three bears. The first two had been an ancient sow with her single cub, perhaps her last, and the third had been a young boar who would not have squared out into anything like a respectable rug. Although probably not more than four years old the boar had been larger by far than the black bear the hunter had previously taken and the guide nearly had to sit on him to keep him from trying for it. The young man later apologized for his sullen reluctance to pass the unworthy bear up. Soon he was feeling rather proud of himself for having done so. By disdaining a mere six-hundred-and-fifty-pound bear he put himself into the big league. True wealth, after all, lies not in the power to amass possessions but to be indifferent to them.

On the morning of their third day they began circling toward the west and before midday found themselves on the edge of a thick growth of alders near a patch of broken ground. The trees themselves and the murky tangle that lay beyond were particularly dense and the guide suggested going around them in the hope of picking up fresh bear sign beyond. There seemed little point in crashing on through without a target to aim for. The noise they would inevitably make would scare anything away and they would be unlikely to spot a bear. The confounding ability of so hulking an animal to remain hidden is one of the great challenges and hazards of brown bear hunting. It is surprising what a man can miss unless a movement happens to arrest his eye.

The weather began to sour as they skirted the wooded area and the guide was half thinking about what they should do if it really turned bad when he spotted some movement about a hundred and fifty feet ahead. They were moving around the thicket on its northern edge when a large pale boar moved out into the open and began casting around for disturbing signals. It seemed to sense danger although it was apparent by its movements that it hadn't quite made up its mind what to do. While the animal was still quartered away from them they side-stepped just enough to be covered by some wind-bent trees and the guide nodded his approval. With infinite care the young man slipped the bolt back about an inch to be certain that he had a chambered shell, eased it forward and checked the safety. The ritual was per-formed in nearly complete silence. All was in order. Three steps to his right would give him a clear shot. All that remained in the balance was his marksmanship.

Trailing his rifle he moved forward in a crouch, came abreast of the opening in the brush, straightened slowly, brought his rifle up, and tucked it in place. He lay the cross hairs on the bear's right shoulder, sucked in his breath, waited for the hairs to center properly a second time and rocked the trigger back with professional ease. The gun roared and the bear went down, a cloud of dust rising from his coat from the impact of the heavy bullet. As soon as the shot went off the guide bounded forward, called for the hunter to follow, and burst out into the open. The wounded bear was bellowing with rage as he fought to regain his feet. It was a pitiful sound, not un-like that of a human being in extreme pain. It was a kind of demented, bawling wail and it penetrated to the very core of the young hunter's not yet insensitive soul.

"His shoulder's broke. Hit him again. Hit him again or you might lose him!" The guide was about ten feet further into the open space than his client. No one will ever know why the young hunter stopped close to the thicket's edge instead of going further out into the open. The guide's position was a better one for a finishing shot. Perhaps the young hunter was stunned by the noise the wounded animal was making. His previous bear had been a clean kill. This animal had been maimed and was bellowing in a furious crescendo of rage. He was fighting to hold himself up, and his moaning and wailing were unrelenting. He was beginning to cast around to seek his tormentor and the guide again called for the finishing shot. When it was slow in coming the guide realized that he might have to end the episode himself. The impending charge could be dangerous. He brought his rifle up, concentrating entirely on the injured bear. If the shot did not come from his left in time, he would finish the bear off himself.

It was because he was concentrating on the wounded bear that the guide didn't see Monarch until it was too late. He heard the hunter's scream and for an instant it crossed his mind that the young man had lost his wits. Then he whirled and saw. For the first moment it looked as if the hunter were patting the bear. His back was to the guide and the giant bear was pressed up against his chest. His hands seemed to be resting on the animal's shoulders. There was no shot. The guide could hit the bear only by shooting squarely at the back of the hunter. It was like watching a nightmarish dance. It was over in an instant, although it seemed like hours.

The hunter had not tumbled to the ground before

Monarch had all but disappeared into the brush from which he had exploded only seconds before. The snap shot the guide managed to get off barely nicked the huge brown rump that was vanishing behind the thick screen. Monarch felt the impact but kept going. When the guide knelt beside the hunter he was weeping. The young man's throat and bottom jaw were missing. The flesh of his chest had been peeled off as if it were clothing and hung in tattered shreds. The guide forgot all about the other bear. It had stopped its search when it couldn't pick up a scent to direct its charge and had half crawled back into the brush where it would die within forty-eight hours. No one will ever know the measure of its agony. The young hunter's wife and children, too, had their special measure of sorrow. The eager young man was the guide's last client.

 18.

THE HUGE BROWN BEARS ARE NOT THE ONLY PREDATORS
on Kodiak Island. It teems with animals locked in an
unending struggle between the killers and the killed.
The prize for skill is survival, the penalty for blundering
is death. The whole system is a delicately balanced scale.
Only nature knows the fulcrum.

The Island consists of three basic arenas: the sky
above, the earth with its freshwater units, and the sea.
Because it is served by distant winds the sky is perhaps
the more apparently dramatic. It is an uncluttered stage

that invites the eye to concentrate on a moving speck. As the great bear emerged from his den for his fourteenth year the invasion of the thermal currents had already begun.

On the day the bear awoke, the magnificent golden eagle arrived. Rare to the Island, he had wintered in Pennsylvania. His powerful three-and-a-half-foot wings had carried him across a vast continent, and in full view of the northward-facing entrance to Monarch's cave he soared and then swooped, in one deft, precise movement, to pluck a mallard from its frantic flight across the open valley. A few feathers drifted to earth and the sepia tiercel vanished over the ridge, piping his absurd little call, his dark head and the amber-brown suffusion on his hindneck feathers distinguishing his kind from all others. His yellow toes with their black talons easily crushed the life from the drake long before he brought it to ground on a rocky prominence. These same talons could have as easily assassinated a wolf. Before eating, the eagle challenged the world once again, his puny call belying his enormous power. The mallard would not be missed. Two hundred thousand wildfowl had wintered on the Island's more sheltered waters. Millions more were on their way.

The buteos came, the buzzard-like rough-legged hawks. One specimen from Ussuriland in Turkestan circled at fifteen hundred feet, eying with interest a similar bird circling at a lower altitude after a journey from New Mexico. Only an expert could say which bird had crossed an ocean and which a continent. The marsh hawks came, the male handsome in his dove-gray finery cast overall with an olive tint, the female distinctive in her darker, gray-brown cast. These hen harriers do not always survive their journeys. Disgruntled farmers blame them for barnyard losses beyond their capacity to inflict and the guns are quick to bark.

The *kyeek, zweeck, kyeek* call marked the end of the osprey's journey from Baja California; the several distinctive calls announced the arrival of the gyrfalcon from Montana, a peregrine falcon from Arizona and a black pigeon hawk from Wisconsin. It was a convocation of pirates, a gathering of hardened killers, who treated one another with respect and deference born of the instinct to survive. With their superb eyesight they watched from the sky as others of their own and related kinds stooped and crushed out the lives of dozens of smaller creatures both feathered and furred.

Not all of Kodiak's aerial raiders came from distant lands. Some had remained throughout the winter and they challenged the visitors with calls and postures no less severe. The northern bald eagle was king when the sun was high; the northern short-eared owl was unchallenged when night shadowed the land. Three lesser birds, although true eaters of meat, avoided the aerial demonstrations of the great raptors. The magnificent black and white magpie, the northern raven and the northwestern crow could not contend but would amount to no less in the final reckoning because of their numbers. They could do with a more varied diet and theirs was an easier life. While the larger predators chal-

lenged each other in acrobatic displays, the less agile
birds stayed near the trees. It wasn't their kind of game.
No less deadly although less conspicuous were the
killers of land-borne habits. The short-tailed weasel,
only recently transformed from an ermine, shot through
tangles that would defy other predators and rode a frantically bucking snowshoe hare to ground amid squeals of
terror and savage fury. The red fox took an indignant
goose by a small inland water hole. The weasel's violent
little mate launched a savagely reckless attack against
an owl, but misjudged her prey and became the victim
herself in the first twenty seconds. Human eyes could
barely have followed the action.

In the streams away from the sea the otter took fish
between games and gambols along muddy banks, and in
more bitter waters the sea otter, possessor of the world's
finest fur, searched for urchins in the deep places where
they flourished. In one day the greatest of all the por-
poises, a killer whale, took four sea otters in a conserva-
tionist's nightmare of carnage. Unsated, the great black
and white hunter cut four fur seals in half before gulp-
ing them down and then for dessert had two hair seals.
His seven-foot dorsal fin flopped over at the tip like a
spaniel's ear.

Over the land the carnage spread. Ground squirrels,
meadow mice, hares and muskrats were served by the
thousands. In the sea fish were consumed by the millions.
The great feasted on the small, the strong and the quick
on the weak and the slow. It was a familiar world into
which Monarch emerged in his sixteenth spring.

No animal seriously challenged the great bear but many vented their anger and voiced their alarm. Wherever he went there were animals to curse and scold him. Some followed him, in the hope of stealing a meal from his leavings, others only because they could not resist the urge to call him one last name.

All over the Island the land was being divided. For almost all of the species involved, territory was essential to nature's ends. There was the nearly universal need to establish first a sacred ground, second a stance of authority, and then, and only then, a liaison that would result in another generation of life to repeat the mystery and reenact the drama. In inland lakes, spiny little sticklebacks stood on their heads and dared others of their kind to approach. Birds postured absurdly, sea animals newly hauled out roared and bellowed along the rocky coasts, fish lashed their tails in a kind of frenzy. Throughout the land the pattern was repeated, with countless variations. Those strong enough to claim a territory that could feed a mate and her young were given the chance to invest their strength and substance with a view to future dividends. Those unable to establish themselves firmly, to claim and hold a piece of one planet out of billions, had their seed dry up within them. Nature despises inferior stock and uses all her wit to deny it access to the future. During the months to come the chocolate boar would frustrate many animals of lesser species. What can a squirrel do if a bear chooses to cross his boundary?

A meteorologist could tell us something about the winds that swept across the spring-gripped land, and the oceanographer something about the rhythm of the waves that worried the beach with energy gathered in distant latitudes. The ornithologist could translate the cries of the birds, and the mammalogists the roars on the seal-breeding grounds along the coast. To the untrained ear, however, the hooting-hissing-whistling-snarling-roaring hum of the land is a symphony, a blend, a special kind of textured order emerging from a special kind of chaos.

The death of a single animal, when witnessed first-hand, can be a saddening thing. One can feel the terror, and unless unfeeling, must wince at the piteous whimpers of the victim in its death throes. For nature, though, there must be a broader canvas and the fact that a life is lived one day, only to be deposited back into the soil the next, is enough. It is self-evident that some chemicals are alive and others not. It is the overall chemistry that matters. As long as the life condition exists, no single life can count unless yet unborn. It is the life that can come as a result of it all, not the life that exists at the moment, that is important to the architect of the life structure.

And so it was another spring. The seeds of the future were given fertile soil. Life as a pulsing, all-pervasive force burgeoned throughout the land and the sea. Movement and color were everywhere. The smallest drama was a part of the largest, the greatest no more important than the least. It was all a part of the whole, and the bear no more than the bee, the fly no less than the eagle played a role. Size was an accident of survival-oriented convenience, might no more than an alternate tool to speed, wit, agility, or stealth.

There was a unique atmosphere to the place and the time, a certain texture, a special smell. There was a sound, there was a feeling, and although it was cosmic in its complexity it was really stunningly simple and compact. It was life, it was spring, it was the time for everything that lived to concentrate on the present and so insure a future. All life was dedicated to a single concept: the future must be served and must come to be. The irony of it all, is that no animal on Kodiak Island — save man — has the capacity to comprehend so profound an abstract. No single creature natural to the Island would hesitate to offer its life to defy anyone or anything that might challenge the future, yet not one could ever know that it existed. Nature, however, did know and as the jealous goddess who ruled over all, she instilled in each the dedication unto death that would assure her and them of immortality.

 19.

AT SEVENTEEN, MONARCH HAD ALL BUT STOPPED GROW-
ing. His weight rose and fell with the seasons, the
texture of his shaggy coat varied according to the time of
year, and there were periods when he seemed bigger
than at others, but basically he had leveled off. Indeed,
a few hairs along the line of his lower lip and others
near the outer corners of his small, intense eyes were
gray at their tips.

In the years of his maturity he had known seven sows
and had fathered fourteen cubs. One mating had pro-

duced a single cub and another triplets. Eleven of the fourteen cubs had survived; two females and one male among his offspring had already reproduced themselves. The chocolate boar was thus immortal.

Despite his advancing years his senses remained sharp. He was still noble breeding stock and worth nature's attention. When he could no longer instill the future with his strength she would dull his senses until they would no longer sustain him. When nature had used him up she would abandon him to perform in solitude his last service within the great cycle: he would die and give his chemistry back to the land. Everything in his physical makeup was on loan, nothing more. Nature may be the creator of all that is beautiful, all that stirs the poet's soul; she may brush our cheeks with gentle summer winds, she may teach the birds to sing and give flowers their perfumed glory. But any sentimentality about these wonders is on the part of the beholder. Nature may be many things, but she is not sentimental. For every life she gives, she demands an ultimate payment in used chemicals. For every life she maintains, she exacts a promise of future life. For her, that is all that matters. Sentimentality is *our* projection, based on our emotional needs. Man is slowly learning not to anthropomorphize, but he may never learn to accord nature the same objectivity. In order to do so he would have to slay a goddess, or at least recognize a queen of his pantheon for what she is.

From our studies of contemporary primitive man, and from our fractional knowledge of ancient man, we can surmise that the hunting of the bear has often had a quasi-religious significance. Man has always coexisted with bears. Assyrian amulets picture the bear wielding a club although the precise significance of the symbol escapes us. The Eskimos within the envelope of their frozen latitudes evolved a bear-god at an early stage of their history and called him Nanuq. Rhpisunt was the bear-mother-goddess of the Haida Indians along the mainland coast not far from Monarch's island range. She was an awesome figure with supernatural powers. When the hunters of the southwestern deserts finally found the elusive House of the Sun they found it guarded by a bear and a serpent. When Estanatlehi, the greatest of the Navajo deities, created new clans to repopulate the world, she sent a bear to them as a protector and as one who could teach them how to hunt. Caves in other parts of the world have yielded stone bear figures, and rock and cave paintings have further attested to the role the great shaggy animal has played in the mysteries of man. The hunter who would take the life of a bear today and ask the taxidermist to create from its salvaged carcass a testimonial of manhood is the inheritor of this ageless magic. His is a ritual honestly come by, surprisingly still extant.

Man has developed the ability, if not the universal will, to control or at least redirect his atavistic drives. And so many men have taken to hunting not to kill, but to record. The hunter with the camera is slowly replacing the hunter with the gun. Theirs is an art requiring the greater skill and in exercising their mastery of it the practitioners often run the greater risks.

The stories of the colossal bear that lived around Deadman Bay had reached the ears of many men. One among them determined to trace the stories to their source, not to cancel its life, but to see it, record it, and experience it as vividly as possible.

The photographer was no less skilled in the ways of the wild than the hunter. His equipment was, if anything, more sophisticated and complex. His Nikon F cameras were the best the genius of the Japanese optical industry had to offer, their many and varied lenses masterpieces of scientific craftsmanship. They had the power to reach out to the bear, snatch away his image, yet deprive him of nothing, and to freeze a moment of his life for posterity. To capture and hold a fraction of cosmic evolution was what fascinated the photographer. He heard and responded to the intriguing if obviously exaggerated tales about the giant bear. He would have him as surely as a hunter, yet he would leave him unharmed.

Monarch had abandoned his habit of approaching campsites. He was no less curious about mankind, but he had become far more cautious. He had reached and passed the point that comes to all great bears who survive their early years; he was a trophy animal of particular interest. When conscious involvement between man and bear becomes mutual, the bear must retreat or perish. Monarch had been tracked so many times, had so often been forced to alter his course because of the scent or sound of man, that he had become hypersensitive. Each of these experiences had been violently disturbing to him, and there had been two bullets to emphasize the lesson he had learned while still a cub with his mother.

Eleven times hunters had actually tracked Monarch's fresh spoor, and eleven times he had outwitted them. On two other occasions he had chosen to stand and fight, although on neither occasion was he their specific target. No experience he had ever had at the hands of man had been rewarding, no contact profitable. He was not really afraid of man, but in the wisdom of his age he generally sought a quick escape when humans arrived and began their blundering invasion of his cherished solitude. It is almost surprising that his victims numbered only two. At least half a dozen times since he had taken a second human life he had been given opportunities to kill again.

In the truly wild places of our planet a guide is needed not only to help the stranger kill, but to save him from being killed. The photographer, like the hunter, needed an expert with him in bear country. The professional welcomed the change. The killing of a bear no longer held any fascination for him and he had come secretly to despise many of the men for whom he worked. He saw in their eyes something he did not like and heard in their voices something he could not fathom. He admired a man who will take a hunter's chances, suffer a killer's hardship, yet will take nothing away from the land. As a man who had himself killed too much, he welcomed this refreshing sanity. However, a bear cannot respond to the gentler nature of the photographer and cannot be relied upon to remain calm simply because he has not been wounded. And so the photographer's guide must carry a rifle.

They were three days' march from the Bay when they first picked up Monarch's spoor. The guide assured his client that no other bear in the area left quite that kind of sign. The enormous hind foot had been planted several inches in front of the forepaw on the right side. Unlike a human foot, the bear's big toe is on the outside, and a track can always be oriented to the bear's position by this means. The tracks that the guide pointed to in the soft mud by the bank of the small inland lake did not differ in kind from other bear tracks they had seen, but they differed dramatically in size. Further on, when they encountered a clear stretch of track, the photographer tried to walk in the bear's footsteps. He had to waddle like a duck, for the side-to-side spread was far greater than a human can comfortably approximate. The photographer tried to emulate Monarch's stride and nearly went flat in the mud. The track sets were fifty-five inches apart.

As they passed beyond the recently flooded area the ground became firm again and they lost the trail in a stretch of exposed rock. The direction the giant had taken seemed clear enough, however, and they continued on until the guide grasped the photographer by the arm and pulled him to a stop. They knelt together beside a clump of brush to examine a recently occupied bed. Moss and leaves had been raked together and a crude mattress formed. The furrows the bear's claws had made in the raking process were still clear on the surrounding ground. As the two men stood and peered intently ahead, the guide slipped the safety off his rifle and moved up until he was abreast of the photographer. "I'll lead from here on in. He might not recognize the fact that you're the friendly type." The photographer fell behind the guide and they started toward the ridge that lay directly ahead.

About ten feet short of the ridge the guide went down on all fours and began creeping forward, always shifting his rifle so that it was ahead of him. The photographer checked the film advance lever on both cameras, depressed the button that allowed the meter to register the light intensity and took a quick reading off an area of neutral density supplied by sun-dried grass. He selected a shutter speed of one five-hundredth of a second to freeze whatever action he might encounter and rotated the stop ring on his lens until the indicator needle settled dead center on the dial. He then moved up to where the guide hunched just below the ridge.

The guide's whisper was clipped and barely audible. "Biggest goddam bear I've ever seen. Just take it slow and he's all yours." The photographer started toward the ridge an inch at a time. He was certain the bear on the other side could hear his heart pounding. He could feel it thudding against his chest wall, noted it pulsing in his right temple. When the downslope was within his range of vision he almost gasped aloud. Monarch was less than twenty-five feet away, methodically digging an enormous hole in the side of the hill. The photographer could sense the guide moving up beside him. Slowly he eased his camera up through the grass until the lens emerged into the clear. Moving with excruciating care, he brought his eye level with the viewfinder. Again with exaggerated slow motion he moved his hand forward and twisted the focusing ring on the lens. He selected the bear's ear as a target and rotated the ring until the two halves were joined in the split-image circle in the center of the viewing field. The whole scene came into focus and the photographer's hand slipped back from the lens to locate the button on top of the camera body.

Monarch had smelled out the new fox den site an hour before and for lack of anything better to do had begun to dig it out. The chances that he would realize any real profit from his labors were slim and yet he dug. As a born plunderer and hopeless drudge it was the kind of simple mechanical activity that he seemed to like. It was repetitive and energy-consuming and satisfied some need within him, a sort of motor response which no one quite understands but which can often be observed and must be significant. Monarch had already moved close to a hundred pounds of dirt when he heard the focal plane shutter slap across within the camera body, giving the sensitive color film its split second of sun. He looked up, sniffed around in a great circle, first facing up the slope and then down.

As he quartered away from the ridge the photographer advanced the film so slowly and deliberately that Monarch missed the slight sound. Momentarily satisfied that he was not in danger, he returned somewhat indifferently to his chores. The second time the shutter slipped past the opening and the reflex mirror swung out of the way, Monarch rose to his hind legs and began to cast around in earnest. The guide alongside the photographer was worried about the short expanse of open land that separated them from the now thoroughly alerted giant. He squeezed the photographer's arm firmly, a signal to hold off until the animal had settled down. One more picture could give their position away and a charge could follow with very little time for a clear, defensive shot. In order to bring his rifle up to ready and still keep the bear in view, the guide would have to reveal himself. He was not anxious to do that.

Monarch woofed several times. Each time the two men could see him hunch and push the sound forth. As long as he was only woofing, the guide felt that things would remain short of the danger point. But if he chopped his jaws just once, or coughed, the guide was determined to shoot. They were too close, the bear too big, and his reputation too bad. For surely this was the bear they called Monarch, the man-killer.

After several minutes of testing the air, the bear sank again to all four feet and shuffled toward his excavation. He was totally uninterested in it now and did no more than push at a little earth before sitting on his heavy haunches to stare down the hill toward the stream and brush that clustered together at the bottom. The afternoon sun slanted across the valley and caught the bear's chocolate fur in its yellowing rays. It was a magnificent moment, one the photographer would probably never know again. He couldn't resist and the shutter and mirror slapped again. In an instant the bear was on his feet facing uphill, thoroughly alert now, and angry.

All of the guide's instincts told him to shoot before the bear could charge, but something held him back. He didn't want to take that life. Something would be destroyed that might never be replaced. This was undoubtedly the outlaw bear, the one men spoke of almost as if he were an ancient legend. A charge seemed imminent and the distance could be covered by the bear on an uphill gallop in a matter of seconds. The hunter didn't even have the advantage of a rifle at the ready. In a way, it was a moment of truth for man and bear alike.

Monarch had located the sound, but the wind was still at his back so he couldn't quite get the scent. If the wind had shifted, his already short temper would have been inflamed by the man-smell and the charge would surely have come. Perhaps because the wind was from the wrong quarter, or for reasons we can never know, Monarch did not charge. He turned instead and shuffled down the hill. When his back was to them the two men eased forward and the photographer got three more shots of the retreating giant. They heard him in the brush after he was lost from view. He ripped a tree to the ground and roared once. Then all was quiet.

Both men sat on the ridge and stared into the little valley. The photographer turned to the guide who was wiping the sweat from the band inside of his cap, "Were you scared?" The guide looked at the man and smiled. "I got an image to maintain." The photographer smiled back and took out his own handkerchief. He felt a slight chill as the perspiration that had soaked his shirt began to evaporate. The wind had shifted and was now blowing from behind them.

 20.

EXPERTS HAVE ESTIMATED THAT KODIAK ISLAND IS SUB-
jected to more hunting pressure per square mile each
year than any other area of equal size on the North
American continent, and perhaps in the whole world.
This pressure, however, is a very recent phenomenon
and nature has not yet had time to make the necessary
accommodations. Nature does not work well when faced
with the need for sudden decisions. She cannot be hurried any more than can her handmaidens, the seasons.
Unless she is given time to review a problem and to ex-

periment with a variety of new ideas at her own method-
ical pace, she shrugs and walks away from a trouble-
some situation, abandoning her perplexed charges to
oblivion. Thus the history of this one planet, at least,
and perhaps of millions of others, is strewn with the
fossilized remains of species caught in changes too swift
or vises too tight. The process of fine adjustment and of
endless experimentation over long periods of time is
called evolution, the result of changes too sudden for
nature to provide for is called extinction.

The Kodiak bear is a species caught in a dangerous
period of transition. He is at the mercy of a distinctly
limited range and of relatively fixed habits. Man, with his
atavistic need for blood, poses a problem for the bear
that may well be insoluble. It could take hundreds or
even thousands of generations for a species of bear to
sharpen its senses in response to the challenge. Up to
now the species of which Monarch was a supreme ex-
ample had no need for such increased capacities. The
capabilities he had were enough for the life nature had
planned for him. No one has yet been able to demonstrate that nature made provisions for her ultimate pri-
mate, the carnivorous, weapon-making, terrestrial ape we
call man. If she did, it would seem a suicidal gesture, the
acting out of a profound death wish. She has seldom
stopped to argue with man. Perhaps his advent has been
too sudden for her, or perhaps she has some supreme
irony up her sleeve.

The Kodiak bear has been able to counter the thrust
of man only by developing more self-protective habits.

Actually, they are nothing more than exaggerations of behavioral equipment that came in the original package. He has not had time for more far-reaching adjustments. The big question (it is the same question to be asked around the world wherever wild creatures still survive) is whether or not any specimens can last long enough to make the necessary adjustments. It could all end with wildlife becoming more and more secretive until the last hidden specimens fade away.

At his peak, Monarch was free of all cares except man. He was attuned to any weather extreme that could befall his home and barely noticed changes in temperature except insofar as they signaled annually renewable behavioral patterns. Beside the salmon stream he was king and as often as not didn't even bother fishing for himself. He would wait until a smaller boar emerged from the stream victorious and then, with a single warning grunt, he would relieve the lesser animal of his catch. The beaches always provided a treasure or two and the berries and the grasses were reliable provender. Only man troubled him and the pressure from that quarter was relentless.

The same hunters returned year after year, determined to persist until the giant bear was theirs. Newcomers arrived each spring and fall, anxious to make a name for themselves by taking the great bear that had defied all others. As much as forty thousand dollars a year was being spent on outfitters, pilots and guides by men for whom Monarch had become an obsession. Not the least important factor was the widely held belief that

Monarch was a vicious killer. If any big bear is a worthy trophy, how much more awe-inspiring is the skin and skull of a killer! How brave the man who could face and conquer so dangerous a monster! How great his service to mankind!

The British engineer, Patterson, earned immortality by ridding East Africa of the man-eating lions of Tsavo, and many white hunters earned nearly equal fame by destroying rogue elephants. Jim Corbett did well in India with tigers and leopards who had developed a taste for human flesh. People still have an almost superstitious admiration for the hunter who can track down and slaughter a dangerous animal.

In few of his contemporary activities does man so graphically betray his emotional origins. Seeking out a bear on his own ground and destroying it comes as close as any ritual on earth to returning man to his earlier state, a nostalgic trip into the past that many men spend a lifetime dreaming about. Ironically, it costs so much to hunt the giant bear that few men can attempt it who have not already shown their worth in jungles of a different sort.

Monarch trudged down through the thicket toward the stream. He had been in the interior valley subsisting on berries, particularly the fall harvest of durable highbush cranberries that could pass through his system virtually unaltered, poque, salmon carcasses on waterways far inland, away from the feverish activity of the lower streams, and dried grass. Since the start of the fall season he had heard the muffled explosions of the hunters' guns and, being unable to locate their points of origin because of the tricks of acoustics over broken ground, he had remained back where he felt secure. Despite his size and strength, he had had two violently painful lessons etched into his flesh and he knew well what the concussive sounds could mean. When a hunting party invaded his valley, he slipped quietly away, leaving the frustrated trackers to speculate on his day-old spoor. For days they would beat their way through exhausting tangles and struggle over ridges of unreliable rock in search of the bear who wasn't there.

In the seemingly aimless way bears have of going about their business, Monarch wandered downstream toward the coast. The late salmon were still running, and the harvest, taken without effort, promised rewards worth claiming.

Twice he had to alter his course when he encountered, in one case, a fresh man-trail, and in another, the sound of men talking. With a well-practiced ease he blended his great bulk back into the woods and silently edged away. Challenges no longer interested him, and he accepted only those which he could not avoid or which caught him during one of those unaccountable cranky spells to which bears are frequently subject. Although the Island supports one bear for every two and a quarter square miles of its area, Monarch encountered few others of his kind, though he often caught their scent. He was known and was given a wide berth.

The brilliantly red sockeye or blueback salmon were still running well in the rushing waters of the lower streams. The most commercially valuable of red salmon meat beneath their glistening skins, they fought their way toward that combination of immortality and oblivion that is the salmon spawning ritual. The three thousand eggs each female would lay would remain dormant until the following spring before hatching. The fry, once loose, would wriggle their way toward lakes and ponds where they would remain for two years or more, feeding on plankton and water fleas. The species is the only one from the entire Pacific world that has left a landlocked variety behind: the one-pound kokanee of lakes no longer open to the sea are sockeye of another era. In his few days by the stream Monarch caught one hundred and fifty salmon, almost all of which had already spawned and were weak and near death. Satisfied, he headed inland again, stopping from time to time to devastate an occasional berry patch.

To the east a magnificent golden eagle had cruised some higher peaks and spotted a white kid, a member of the Island's small herd of mountain goats. Above the prominence the great bird had circled and, when the moment seemed right, had plummeted toward the unsuspecting kid. In a moment the collision would catapult the young goat over the cliff to its death and there on the broken rocks below, the eagle would feed on the broken white body of its victim. But the adults of the herd were alert and at the last moment the eagle had to swerve in order to avoid impact with the larger animals, heavy, pointed-horned goats not likely to tumble over the edge, who could stand and hold and cause the eagle the greater harm.

Furious, the raider rose in a wide, sweeping circle, screaming her absurd little cry, perhaps warning the herd below that she would be back and claim her due another day. The eagle failed, on this occasion, and the kid learned a valuable lesson; beware of shadows that scud across the rocks too fast.

Circling toward the south and west the eagle spotted another meal. With great powerful beats she rose on a convenient thermal and when high enough for her purpose dropped with swift and deadly aim. The yearling buck was carried to earth by the force of the impact and barely had time to realize its plight before the eagle's talons closed beneath its backbone to sever the spinal cord.

The golden eagle spread her wings across the carcass of her victim and threw her head back, her wicked jaws agape. Turning her head slowly from side to side she issued once again her unimpressive call. Volume or not, the world had been warned that the giant bird was upon her kill and all others should give way. She stood there as if transfixed, her enormous wings blanketing her victim in a lustrous, feathery shroud.

Monarch had stood in the brush beside the clearing, sensing the deer's presence and trying to decide whether or not to stalk it when the eagle fell and settled the question. The colliding bodies, the rustle of feathers, and the eagle's cry all carried clearly to him in the wings. As the eagle prepared to feed, Monarch stepped out onto the stage.

He was no more than halfway clear of the brush before the incredibly sharp-eyed bird had his measure and flew into a monumental rage. Her brown eyes glistened with fury and her yellow toes rolled back, extracting her talons from the deer's flesh. The lanceolate feathers, deep brown suffused with amber and tipped with pale tan, rose and her wings moved out from her body. With a rage known to her ancestors during the Oligocene thirty-six million years ago and unblunted by time, she faced a foe sixty-four times her own weight. With her hackles up and her wings brought forward, hunched like a football player's shoulders, she was astonishingly formidable. He was the intruder, plodding and determined; her rage was the greater.

She thrust her head forward and called, then hissed a final warning. He continued his advance, his head low and swaying with each measured step. Her fury mounted until it was blind, without reason, and although it was too late for her to realize it, without hope.

When Monarch was twenty feet from the bird and her kill, she rose into the air and came down again ten feet to the side of the arena's center. Lathered to distraction, she watched the great lumbering bear approach her kill, and when finally able to stand the insult no longer, she rose again and with her talons thrust forward launched herself at the bear in a suicidal plunge that took even him by surprise. Just before she struck, his forepaw shot out and pinned the golden bird to the ground. Her talons sank into his leg in one last convulsive gesture of hatred before her life was expunged. She died locked in his flesh, the tips of her talons touching bone. Monarch raised his paw and shook but the eagle would not come loose. He shook again and finally sat back on his rump and tore the crushed eagle free with his teeth. The bird's final act left gaping holes in his leg and his limp would be pronounced for weeks to come.

Before leaving the clearing he fed on both the bird and the deer. Toward the end of his feast he heard gunfire in the distance and took off without bothering to cache the remains.

At best, man is a blunderer in the woods. He smells, he talks, and he has forgotten how to walk quietly. Twigs snap under his feet and little branches clatter against his guns, cameras, binoculars and clothing. Monarch could read all of these signs as if they were posted warnings.

Here is the irony in the play between the human hunter and his quarry: man, in his rise from animal beginnings, has retained the desire, perhaps the need, to kill, but has forfeited that skill in favor of more usable intellectual gifts. His drive to kill may be instinctual, but he has lost the operational instincts that support it. The bear, though, has no such conscious desires. On any intellectual level, the bear hardly rates a nod compared with his human foe, yet the bear can outwit men most of the time. He has retained his instincts and these are able to accept the acquired knowledge of the individual animal and make of the combination a skill that man can never achieve. The hunt, then, is a contest between atavistic desire and intellectual analysis on the one hand, and instincts suffused with shadow-learning on the other. It is a scale that tips in favor of the latter combination in most individual encounters. For entire species, though, the scale goes the other way. Bears are not numerous and man's biological potential is limitless. There are fewer than two thousand Kodiak bears alive in the world today as opposed to thousands of millions of men. The game is rigged and the bear can never overcome the house odds.

Sublimely unaware of these abstract considerations, Monarch lived out his life. The years rolled off him like the rains that fell on his Island home. He would shuffle into a fog patch in a stunted alder growth one year, and emerge on the far side a year later. He was a ghost, an evolutionary holdover from another age, a mass of chemicals gathered up from the soil and infused temporarily with life, a speck of dust within a cosmos. About his ways he went, lost from all view most of the time, infuriatingly tantalizing when seen.

Seen or unseen, he was a challenge simply because he existed. He would have gladly snuffed out the life of any man he could conveniently smash to earth and if he had followed the pattern of some others of his kind, he would probably have eaten some of the flesh then available to him if left undisturbed. He would more gladly, however, avoid man, given the chance, but such was not to be his lot. He was to be pursued as long as he lived. He could make his peace with man only by dying.

For Monarch, though, each day was new and all memories were lost until summoned up briefly by a familiar combination of signals to instruct him. He was as unconscious of his experiences five minutes after they were past as he was of time itself. In his moments of repose his relaxation was magnificent, unlike anything the troubled mind of man could ever allow its host. Beneath his semiconscious state there lay, however, a cunning and a savage skill. Monarch was a volcano, both in size and power, waiting for external stimulation. Left alone, he would be forever quiet within. But Monarch's kind is almost never left alone.

 21.

THE LOW SHALE CLIFFS AND MEANDERING SHORELINE OF
Deadman Bay became Monarch's stronghold. Perhaps it
was the familiar aspect of the area or perhaps it was something else about the region that appealed to him. Most
of his early years had been spent on these raw, damp
shores, and within a few miles of the sedge tide flats
around the Bay's perimeter he had learned some of his
hardest lessons. He had feasted hugely on the crystal
springs that roll into the Bay from the hills, for here
were the rich salmon streams with their pea-sized gravel

banks. In this district he had grown from a cub who lost his salmon catch to his elders to the mammoth he now was.

Monarch would have been well advised to leave the area, for it was one of the most heavily hunted on the whole Island. The White Hills behind the Bay were and are known to all hunters who study the Island's potential as a likely spot where a man can get his bear. Yet this was Monarch's country, and although he might wander away from it, he always returned. It was as if he were on a long tether. He might roam in a sweeping arc at the end of his lead, but he always ended up back at the stake in the center.

Familiar and reliable feeding sites are important to a bear. Anything that simplifies his life will attract him. Monarch knew which were the first slopes to be free of snow and knew where the first asparagus-like hellebore shoots would appear beneath the cover of leaves and humus. He knew, too, where to seek the spring harvest of nettle and the beach rye, and the twisted stalk and crowberries under the summer sun. He knew the salmon streams and the high meadows where the sassy ground squirrels could be had. Aside from the probable comfort he found in general familiarity, it was probably this reliable provender as much as anything else that brought him back to familiar trails. It is not always pleasant country and the sun shines no more than fifty percent of the time each year, yet it is that very rainfall, the dampness that is always present, that provides the cornerstone for the vast food store bears must have.

Monarch stumped down through a patch of cotton-woods, crossed a small well-known clearing and entered a stand of evergreens. He was in no hurry; he appeared to be moving almost as the contour of the ground directed him. The area was quiet, for the spring hunting was over and his hide could not be legally sought again until October. He remained alert, however, for the man-smell was always there, frequently encountered. He could not understand that the summer brought only harmless tourists, more each year, who came simply to look and to photograph.

Near the edge of a cedar stand he came upon a well-used tree. The ground around it was worn flat and its bark was badly scarred. Vertical tooth marks were plainly evident where another large bear had recently been at work. As if in defiance Monarch rose to his hind legs and bit into the bark further up the trunk than the other bear had been able to reach. The syrupy sweetness followed by the turpentine aftertaste pleased him and he grunted with pleasure. Thrusting his abdomen against the tree he began moving up and down in a sensual sort of way. He rolled his head back, listened for a moment to reassure himself, and then began rocking back and forth, scratching his stomach and leaving small tufts of his fur clinging to the ragged bark. Satisfied, he sat down heavily on his rump and began scratching every available part of his body that his front and hind claws could reach. He cooed to himself and only occasionally stopped for a quick check of his surroundings. Finally he stood and turned his back to the tree and rocked rhythmically. This was the most absurd display of all. For a full ten minutes he rubbed his enormous rump against the tree. His exertions were so vigorous that before he was done he had worn smooth spots on his hide. With the sheer physical gratification of it all he rolled his eyes, uttered an entire range of contented sounds and drooled pools of saliva onto the ground. It was the hot and itchy time and the hedonist in him dictated his actions. A bear may not be the clown some people think he is, but he can act it at times.

As midafternoon approached Monarch began looking for a comfortable place to lay up for a few hours of rest. As he was settling himself in the damp earth beneath a windfall he heard the unmistakable sounds of a cub in trouble. The bawling and wailing carried to him from an adjacent valley. He could not resist the sounds and, as much a prisoner of his curiosity as he had been as a cub himself, he began heading in the direction of the disturbance. As he passed over the low intervening ridge a growl built up in his throat, an involuntary response to the sounds of the cub. Below him he could hear human voices. Four men were gathered around an eight-foot section of 14-gauge culvert pipe that had been anchored to some stout trees near a stream. A drop-door made from quarter-inch steel sealed the four-foot opening at the end of the pipe and inside, the prisoner, a yearling cub, bawled incessantly. His lament stopped shortly after a nylon syringe was thrust through a hole in the side of the pipe on the end of a pole and was jabbed into his rump. Once he was immobilized, the anesthetized cub was dragged from the pipe, subjected to a series of examinations, and was then finally tagged.

Meanwhile Monarch paced back and forth in the brush just below the ridge and mumbled to himself. He had no sympathy for the cub; indeed, he would probably have killed and perhaps even eaten it if given the chance to do so, but the men angered him, as they always did.

On the far side of the small valley the cub's mother hung back in a stand of trees, lathering herself into a fury, but she did not have the courage to charge. When she had shown herself at the first calls of distress, she had been driven back by firecrackers thrown in her direction. One man had burst a charge under her nose by firing a projectile from a 12-gauge shotgun.

Having grumbled enough, and being unwilling to expose himself to the men below unless forced to a showdown, Monarch slunk off. He grumbled once again when he crossed the familiar spoor of the copper boar that had been his special foe since their encounter on the seaweed flat nearly two decades earlier. The lighter and only slightly smaller boar had survived despite his mutilated right forepaw and the loss of his right ear and left eye, souvenirs of another encounter with Monarch. He always managed to avoid his ancient enemy although they were often in the same territory at the same time and usually about the same business. This was the third time in two weeks that Monarch had come across the antagonizing spoor. It never failed to elicit the same angry response, yet he never really followed it up or attempted to bring about another showdown.

Monarch bred again that year, selecting for his mate a seven-year-old sow of less than average size. Their idyll lasted for three weeks and a few days and was terminated without ceremony or sentiment, just as had all the others. Long before the crisp, early days of fall he was solitary again. His arrival at the salmon stream was leisurely, for he had no need to establish a place for himself or to contend for a better spot. He would take whatever he wanted whenever he arrived.

Tiring of the confusion and noise of the salmon stream after several days, Monarch wandered off by himself to the quiet and solitude he seemed to cherish above all else. Other animals, even other bears whom he could easily dominate, made him nervous.

The day after he abandoned the stream he was on the beach. He hung back in the brush for the first day, disturbed by two small boats that were plying back and forth in the inlet. By the second day he was used to the sounds they made and moved out onto a flat of slippery seaweed as the tide rolled back toward the sea. He was spotted at a distance of nearly half a mile, and a 1000-millimeter reflex lens hastily fastened to a tripod with a camera hanging off the back focused on him and recorded his image in color, and then in black and white. At that distance he was not recognizable as any particular bear, only as an animal of exceptional size. The husband-and-wife schoolteachers from Minnesota were thrilled with their "catch" and forgot momentarily about the amount of money their trip was costing them.

Back in the woods, Monarch again came upon the spoor of the copper boar, and again he voiced his extreme displeasure. After casting about for a few minutes he tramped off into dense cover, where he slept for a little less than an hour. He was moving again while the sun was still high and entered a small, stream-cut hollow several miles from the beach. Suddenly, warned by one sense or another, he was up on his hind legs, testing the wind for urgent messages. Men were close, very close. His anger flared.

The winds in the small depression were uncertain and he could not locate the source of his uneasiness. He was unwilling to depart without being able to pick his direction with care. He went down again to all fours and got behind a windfall. The scent was still there, but no noise. He waited, expecting to hear human sounds, but none came. The tension mounted and with it his fury. The scent was so close that he found it impossible to remain still and moved again, out between two trees. He felt the small pain almost simultaneously with the first noise he could distinguish as foreign. He spun to face his unknown foe, but it was too late. His hind legs would not respond, then his forequarters gave out. For the first time since reaching maturity, Monarch of Deadman Bay was helpless. The dart had been fired from a CO_2 powered rifle and had caught him squarely in the rump. Upon contact the automatic syringe had discharged more than 100 milligrams of the drug into his system. It was not a large enough dose to paralyze him completely, but he was helpless. His hind legs twitched and his shoulders hunched forward, then relaxed. His eyes remained open and he could hear the men talking as they stood off and waited for the drug to take full effect. He could not appreciate their admiring remarks.

Finally, satisfied that the succinylcholine had provided them with sufficient protection, the men moved in. At their first touch, Monarch twitched and fought valiantly to regain his feet, but was unable to so much as lift his head from the ground. He was forced to tolerate their handling and barely felt the second needle enter his intraperitoneal cavity. In a few moments he was totally anesthetized and the biologists began their rapid series of tests.

While one biologist inserted a thermometer into the drugged bear's rectum, another made an impression of his teeth. A third drew a hefty blood sample and then began a gross examination of his general condition. His fur was inspected for external parasites, the wound on his chest was duly recorded on his register card, and he was checked for other wounds or signs of combat. One of his two bullet wounds, the one in his shoulder, was found and recorded, and his eyes, nostrils and ears were checked, again for parasites, and a mucous specimen was obtained. One of the biologists again commented on his extreme size and openly wondered whether or not he was the fabled man-killer so often discussed back in town. He was photographed as he lay and then the team took a break. One, a student on his first big-game survey, sat on Monarch's rump as he lighted his cigarette. A fellow student photographed him in that pose and jokingly offered to sell him wallet-sized prints at a reduced rate for a dozen or more. A senior member of the team suggested that it was time to head back to camp and the students began packing their equipment and specimens into their containers.

When everything was packed and ready, the leader of the team administered the antidote with a six-inch needle. It broke, and was extracted with a small pair of pliers. A second needle was fitted and the drug injected.

The biologists were some distance away before the antidote began to take effect. The leader had been nearly mauled by a bear some years earlier when he remained near it too long after administering the antidote. With the safety of his team members foremost in his mind he was in the habit of clearing out before the bears they examined were fully conscious and usually very angry.

At first, Monarch was aware of a slight buzzing noise, and then light penetrated to the black limbo into which the anesthesia had thrust him. He still could not move, still had no physical sensation of self, but the outside world began to have fractional meaning for him. He heard the brush move, but could not respond. He was neither angry nor frightened. He lay temporarily suspended between the real world and that which had been fabricated for him in distant laboratories and chemical plants. His sense of smell was returning, but he was still too confused by what had happened to be able to make any distinctions. He drooled copiously and made small, ineffectual sounds. He tried to roll his head, but couldn't summon the strength. His limbs twitched and shuddered, but his coordination had not yet returned. He was minutes away from being able to stand. The dose of pentobarbital sodium had been too massive; his great size had prompted the scientist to take too much of a precaution.

The copper male had heard the sounds of the departing biologists as they crossed his trail about twenty yards ahead of him. He swung off into the brush and circled around behind them. He came upon Monarch while the giant was still trying to focus in on the world around him. At first the copper male's instincts told him to retreat. He recognized his foe immediately, and his natural response was to withdraw. But something was different this time.

Slowly he approached his hated rival, the great chocolate boar that had condemned him to live his life as a cripple, a secondary force despite his own great size.

Confused as he was, Monarch recognized his archenemy. Something between a roar and a screaming whine filled his throat as he managed to extend his forelegs. He pushed the front half of his body up and rocked uncertainly, struggling to coordinate the effort with his hindquarters. Chomping his jaws and drooling, he thrust his head forward and with a deep grunt managed to get the back part of his enormous body into a semicrouch. He wavered for a moment, just a moment, before the copper male struck. Monarch rolled over, first onto his side and then over onto his back. For a moment his four legs pointed straight up. The blow from his eleven-hundred-pound rival winded him badly and he was flailing, trying to adjust his limbs and his senses at the same time. He rocked over onto his side again with a heaving moan but it was too late.

The copper boar had passed completely over Monarch on his first thrusting charge. His momentum carried him ten feet beyond, where he hauled up and turned. His jaws were chomping furiously too; he was in a transport of rage. He paused for a moment, unable to comprehend Monarch's plight. He was waiting for the countercharge that could never come. Seizing the initiative once more, he struck again, this time fatally. As powerfully built as Monarch was, he couldn't withstand the massive blow in the neck, not without being able to brace himself. The huge paw came down behind his ear as the copper boar sank his fangs into his exposed shoulder. For several minutes the huge animal tore at Monarch, clawing and biting, and the noise was horrendous. It was all unnecessary. Monarch had died seconds after he received the blow in the neck. But the last shudders, those last few spastic reflexive tremors that ran through his dead body, served to enrage the copper boar even more. When at last he backed off, his head held low and sounds of fury still issuing from his throat, Monarch was a bloodied, almost unrecognizable hulk. In a last gesture of disdain the copper boar moved forward again and began to feed. Several crows and half a dozen magpies waited on nearby branches. Others began to arrive.

The copper boar did not bother to cache what remained of Monarch. He moved out of the valley and was never seen in the district again.

As for Monarch, he had paid his final debt. In bird droppings and bear scats, between the pincers of beetles and ants, his chemicals were broken down and slowly returned to the land. These chemicals would enrich the soil and help to grow the plants that had nourished the bronze sow when she had carried Monarch and his sister within her many years before. The hunters that came to seek him in the years that followed would miss him, but the life systems of Kodiak Island would not. He was where he ultimately belonged, back in the cycle, back again in time.